THE SPANIARD'S
PLEASURABLE
VENGEANCE

THE SPANIARD'S PLEASURABLE VENGEANCE

LUCY MONROE

MILLS & BOON

First published in Great Britain 2018
by Mills & Boon, an imprint of HarperCollins*Publishers*
1 London Bridge Street, London, SE1 9GF

Large Print edition 2019

© 2018 Lucy Monroe

ISBN: 978-0-263-08198-5

Printed and bound in Great Britain
by CPI Group (UK) Ltd, Croydon, CR0 4YY

For my readers, because you've stuck with me through the challenges that make writing so hard. Your letters reminded me that my stories touched real people's hearts and that is why I write—so, thank you! I am so grateful to each of you who picks up a book and completes the circle of connection to me, the author, and especially thankful for the readers who have encouraged me through some of the most difficult times in my life.

I write for all of you.

PROLOGUE

"I DON'T NEED a damn appointment! I'm his sister, you cretin." The sharp American accent and strident tone of Gracia's voice reached Basilio through his partially closed office door.

The heavy door opened forcefully, slamming back against the rich paneling of his wall, but surprisingly, his administrative assistant made it into the office a step ahead of Basilio's sister. "Sir, I'm sorry." The distress at not holding her post was clear in his admin's tone. "She refused to even wait for me to ascertain if you were still on your conference call."

Gracia came storming around his admin at the same time as his executive assistant came rushing in from her annex office.

"What is going on in here?" Her hair in a severe chignon, her navy business suit immaculate, his fifty-year-old executive assistant could do freezing aristocratic disapproval better than even Basilio's mother, who was actually the daughter of a count.

His admin immediately began apologizing again as he stood from his desk, giving his sister a look that would have made Basilio's mother proud. Gracia halted in her approach to his desk, her annoyed expression morphing to one of consternation.

She gave the EA a moderately polite look before looking at Basilio with wariness. "It is a family emergency."

Basilio merely waited in silence for more information.

His executive assistant wasn't so patient. "I see, and there was no time for you to call and apprise us of your imminent arrival so we could clear your brother's schedule on your drive from the airport?" Camila Lopez asked with clear censure.

Gracia looked between Basilio and his EA, her cheeks going pink. "I wasn't thinking of calling. Only getting here."

"And if *Señor* Perez had been away from the office?" Camila pressed with a single raised, perfectly shaped black eyebrow.

"I didn't think of that."

As amusing as he found his sister's interaction with his executive assistant, Basilio did not have time for the entertainment. He did, in fact, have a very busy day.

"Thank you for your assistance and I will need the next thirty minutes for Gracia," he said to both his admin and Camila. "See that we are not disturbed."

"Of course, *señor*," Camila said to him with just the right amount of deference before offering his sister a look that said clearly, she wasn't worried about someone *else* interrupting.

Once the other two women had left his office, both doors through which they'd gone closed firmly behind them, Basilio indicated one of the chairs facing his desk. "Sit down, Gracia, and tell me what has you forcing your way past my admin."

Gracia sank into the seat with more grace than her behavior had shown so far. "It really is a family emergency, Baz."

For the family that so rarely remembered he was a member?

"Explain," he demanded as he settled back into his own chair.

Gracia frowned at his tone. "You remember when that awful teenager hit little Jamie with her car?"

"I am unlikely to forget." Five years before, his then four-year-old nephew had spent two weeks in a coma after being hit by a car while on an outing with his mother.

"Well, apparently, she changed her name and moved away from Southern California."

"Unsurprising." While Basilio had been in Spain at the time, saving his father's company from bankruptcy, he knew that Miranda Weber had been vilified in the broadcast media and even worse on all the social media outlets.

"Yes, well. Some idiotic reporter found out who she is and is resurrecting the story."

And this was the family emergency that she needed Basilio's help with? When usually both Carlos and Gracia were happy to forget they were half siblings most of the time.

Putting aside his own sense of cynicism about their definition of family, Basilio said, "I can see where that would be emotionally difficult for Carlos and Tiffany."

"Yes. It's awful! And this time some fly-by-night morning gossip show wants to interview the girl. She's all set to give them her side of the story."

"She's not a girl any longer, surely." Miranda had been nineteen five years ago.

"Woman, then," Gracia said dismissively. "She'll go on television and lie. About our family!"

"Surely Carlos has PR people who can handle this." Not to mention lawyers. If the woman lied in a public forum, they could bring a civil suit.

"You know he prefers you call him Carl."

Yes, because it was less Spanish, letting him forget he ever had a father named Armand Perez. "That is what you want to discuss now?" Basilio asked, his voice dry.

"No, of course not." Gracia wrung her hands. "It's just you have to do something!"

"What do you imagine I can do that Carl and Tiffany cannot? They are not exactly without resources." Carlos's wife came from an old and wealthy East Coast family.

Basilio's brother ran his stepfather's business, one of respectable enough size to have public relations people on retainer. While Perez Holdings was much bigger and more successful now, that had not always been the case.

"She had a restraining order taken out against both Carl and Tiffany. It includes any representative working for, or on retainer from, them."

"How did she manage that?" Basilio wondered aloud.

"It's insane, I know."

That was not what Basilio had meant. For Miranda Weber to obtain such a thing, serious threats had to have been made. Cursed with a deep-seated sense of entitlement, his brother could be a hothead, as well. Carlos had never had to save a company, or put the hours into shoring up his family's name in the international community as Basilio had done. When their father split with Carlos and Gracia's mother, she'd remarried quickly and both of Basilio's older siblings had embraced their new American family wholeheartedly, taking their stepfather's last name and rejecting their Spanish heritage for their American mother's way of life.

While Basilio was not sure he could blame Carlos, considering the current circumstances, clearly the older man's temper and certainty he could do as he pleased had cost him access to Miranda.

When Basilio didn't say anything right away, Gracia added, "I think it might have been her brother-in-law or something."

"She has a sister?" He didn't remember that. He'd thought the woman who put his nephew into a coma was an only child.

"Apparently. Only a half sister, but still…"

"Yes, still." Basilio knew just how little regard his sister and brother had for the concept of a half sibling.

"Oh, get off it, Baz. I didn't mean you."

"As you say."

Gracia leaned forward. "You need to do something."

"What would you have me do?"

"Well, Carl's company doesn't have quite the sway yours does."

That was an understatement. Basilio had ruthlessly built Perez Holdings into a powerful multibillion-dollar international entity, while his brother's realty group was worth mere millions. "The Madison Realty Group is hardly a global concern" was all Basilio said, though.

"Exactly."

"So?" Basilio prompted.

Gracia's expression turned crafty. "So, maybe you can convince the brother-in-law to withdraw his support."

"Who is this in-law?"

"His name is Andreas Kostas. That's Greek, isn't it? I don't remember the name of his company."

Surprise made Basilio sit up straighter in his chair. "Yes, it is Greek, and I know exactly who he is. My company uses his company's security software, or what used to be his company. I believe he recently merged with Hawk Enterprises."

Andreas Kostas was a shark's shark and he was

now in business with one of the biggest sharks swimming in their waters. No wonder Carlos needed help dealing with Miranda's family.

Gracia waved that information away. "Whatever. He didn't respond well when Carl contacted him, hoping to convince him to talk Miranda out of doing the interview."

"If he threatened him, I don't imagine so." Kostas wasn't known for tolerating fools or blowhards. Unfortunately, Carlos had played both on occasion.

"Who said Carl threatened anybody?" Gracia sounded indignant, but her guilty expression didn't jibe with her words.

Basilio just gave his sister a look until she squirmed in her chair.

"Okay, he may have said some things he didn't mean, but come on." Gracia waved her hands in agitation. "He and Tiffany went through enough five years ago."

"On that we can agree."

"So, you'll do something?"

"I will come to the States and look into the situation." That was all he would promise.

If it came down to it, Basilio wasn't above using his influence and power to push either Andreas Kostas or his sister-in-law into doing what was best for Basilio's family because for him family came first, last and always. However, first he would get some real answers about what was going on.

"You have to hurry. She's slated to do her interview in three weeks. The recent media storm is just starting to die down, and if she does that interview, it's bound to blow everything up again."

"Understood. What name does she go by now?"

"She kept her first name, but changed Weber to Smith."

"Very anonymous."

Gracia's lips twisted in distaste. "Yes."

Well, Weber or Smith, Basilio had every intention of finding the woman who had already cost his family so much. Whatever it took, he would protect the brother and sister-in-law who had suffered enough.

CHAPTER ONE

LATE FOR DINNER with her newfound sister and recently acquired brother-in-law, Randi rushed out of her even more recently acquired office.

She'd been shocked and delighted when Kayla asked Randi if she was interested in taking over managing responsibilities for Kayla's for Kids, the shelter her sister had founded for at-risk children and youth. The opportunity to do what Randi loved while living near enough to get to know her long-lost sister had been too good to pass up. Besides, she got to use both her degree in business and adjunct degree in social services.

Part of her new job would include launching a second site in the western suburbs of Portland. Apparently, Andreas had donated enough for the expansion as a wedding gift, in addition to designating his new company's charitable contributions all to Kayla's for Kids, making fund-raising efforts a lot less stressful for Randi's team.

It was Randi's dream job and she adored her sister and brother-in-law for making it possible.

Collision with a hard, muscular wall on the sidewalk abruptly halted Randi's headlong flight to her car.

She cried out and then immediately started apologizing, even as she felt her balance waver. "I'm so sorry! I didn't see you."

Big, strong hands on her upper arms stopped her bounce backward that would have landed Randi on her backside. "Is that a common occurrence, running into people you didn't see?" he asked, a foreign accent subtle but unmistakable.

Randi winced. The man could not know the old wound his words bled yet again.

She pulled herself together with a firm mental yank and shrugged. "I'd love to say *no*, but I have a tendency toward klutziness, especially when I'm in a rush."

Why she was admitting that particular failing to this gorgeous man, she did not know. Because man, total hottie alert. Easily as tall as her brother-in-law, who stood at six feet four inches, the black-haired man with sexy stubble on his face towered over Randi's own five feet five inches.

Espresso-brown eyes locked on hers. "I see. Are you in a rush often?"

For whatever reason, she didn't step back from him. "Not really, just sometimes. Though it's usually walls I run into, or doorjambs, or you know, furniture. I hardly ever bump into people."

Even, white teeth flashed in a smile that didn't quite reach his dark brown eyes. "I'm special, then."

"You could take it that way, yes."

He released her arms. Finally, but he did not step out of her personal space. "I believe I will."

"Okay." Heat climbed up her neck and into her cheeks that Randi could do nothing about.

He offered his hand. "Basilio Perez."

"Oh, um, Randi Smith." She laid her palm against his.

Instead of shaking hands, he lifted hers to his lips, brushing a barely there kiss on the backs of her knuckles. "Nice to meet you, Ms. Smith."

Randi finally understood what it meant to be electrified by a man's touch. His lips against her skin sent frissons of sensation throughout her body and she gasped.

"Ms. Smith? Are you all right?" There was something in his too-knowing gaze that said he was perfectly aware of the effect he was having on her.

She tried to speak, then cleared her throat and tried again. "Randi, please."

"Randi is short for?"

"Oh, um, no one ever asks. They just ask stuff like if I enjoy having a boy's name."

"So?" He hadn't let go of her hand and he now brushed his thumb over her knuckles, where his lips had been.

She had no thought of not answering. "Miranda."

"Lovely name."

"You think so?" She'd always found it old-fashioned.

"I do."

"Basilio is pretty neat, too. Spanish?" she guessed.

"You got it in one. My friends call me Baz."

"My friends call me Randi."

"I prefer Miranda."

Did that mean he didn't want to be friends? Only he'd implied she should call him *Baz*. "Are we going to be friends?"

"I would like that."

Good. "Me, too. I mean…" But she wasn't sure what she'd meant to say, the sexual chemistry between them playing havoc with the efficient firing of synapses in her brain.

"I hope you mean just that."

"Yes, okay."

"So, dinner tonight?" he asked, still caressing her hand.

"I have plans with my sister and brother-in-law." And as much as she wanted to spend time with her sister, giving up a date with such a delicious man was hard.

"After-dinner drinks?"

"Really?" Oh, man, why had she asked that? "I mean, that would be great. Fine."

She was just going to sink into the sidewalk right now.

"When and where?"

She thought about the location of the restaurant she was supposed to meet her family at and a likely spot near it. "How about the piano bar at the Heathman?"

It was quiet, with lots of places to sit in an intimate *tête-à-tête*.

"Fine. What time?" Basilio asked.

"Eight o'clock?" She was having an early dinner with Kayla and Andreas.

"Perfect. I will get my own dinner and meet you there."

Taking a risk, Randi asked, "You could join us?"

"You are sure I would not be an unwelcome intrusion?"

She loved the formal cadence of his speech, so different from her own. "Not at all. I'm sure Kayla and Andreas would not mind at all."

But she'd better call and give a heads-up on her way over.

"Then I would be pleased to accept."

"Great. Um, you can meet me there?"

"Naturally. I would not expect you to get into a car with a stranger after such short acquaintance."

And why she wished she could, she wasn't even going to think about. Ever since the trouble five years before, Randi had become very wary of new people and even making friends, much less dating. But no way was this man a grubby reporter, looking for lascivious details from the years-old tragedy.

Not in his five-thousand-dollar suit and shoes that probably cost more than she made in a week.

They made arrangements to meet at the restaurant in twenty minutes. Then Randi was running for her car, even later than she had been.

* * *

Basilio pulled into the valet parking for the Heathman.

A walk from the restaurant to the piano bar would be further opportunity to draw out Miranda Smith née Weber. Bumping into her on purpose had made two things very clear. One, the picture in the file he'd had compiled on her did not capture the sweet naïveté she wore like a cloak, nor her unconscious sensuality. Two, seduction might well be his best course of action in achieving the goal his family needed.

While intimidation tactics were not yet off the table, he had a feeling using the instant attraction between them would be more easily effective.

Walking into the restaurant a few minutes later, he was once again struck by the clarity of her gray eyes as they met his across the roomful of diners in the upscale steak house. Even in the subdued lighting of the restaurant, the gray orbs glowed. Miranda was sitting with Andreas Kostas and another woman with eyes the exact color and vibrancy of Miranda's, declaring her the sister.

Basilio allowed the maître d' to lead him across the restaurant to the linen-clad table for four. Appetizers and bread were already on the table, indicating the Kostases had been there for a while.

Miranda stood up. "You made it."

Basilio nodded, finding her enthusiasm almost charming. There was such an innocence about this woman, he found it hard to believe she had plans to blow his family's peace right out of the water. She did not look or behave like someone who would go on a talk show to spite them, particularly after committing such a heinous act as hitting a small child with her car.

But he had it on good authority that Miranda Smith, for all her airs of innocence, was exactly that kind of woman.

He could not afford to forget that fact.

"This is my sister, Kayla Kostas, and her husband, Andreas." Miranda indicated the other two people with one hand, nearly knocking over a filled water goblet.

Her brother-in-law saved the table from getting doused with a discernible lack of impatience.

Basilio inclined his head to the married couple. "It is a pleasure to meet you."

"Randi said she met you on the street?" Kayla asked as Andreas sat down, clearly wanting more information.

Miranda had dropped back into her chair across the dining table from him. She smiled shyly at him, her cheeks tinged with color. Was she embarrassed she'd allowed him to pick her up?

He winked at her and watched the color darken along her lovely cheekbones, then turned his head to meet Kayla's eyes. "We bumped into each other."

"More like I mowed him down in my rush to be on time."

The twinge he felt that she was taking responsibility for the collision he had orchestrated was odd, and Basilio ignored it. "You were in a rush to get here, I believe."

"I was late."

"I guessed."

She ducked her head. "Yes, well…"

"Do you make a habit of picking up women you bump into on the street?" Andreas asked, his tone cynical.

"Having dinner with a beautiful woman is never a hardship." Basilio met the assessing green gaze steadily.

He'd spent years rebuilding his father's company and the Perez name in business circles. Basilio had learned long ago not to allow anyone else's opinion of him, or his actions, to disconcert him.

Andreas Kostas was not the only dangerous business shark in the room.

"You didn't answer my question." The other man was not easily fobbed off.

Basilio didn't mind. "I did not."

He was going to leave it that way until he noted the uncertainty clouding Miranda's expression. His plans required her trust.

So he spoke to her, not the nosy Greek sitting to Basilio's left. "I have never picked up a woman I met on the street. I did not pick you up like a lost puppy. I asked you for drinks. You suggested dinner and I was pleased to accept."

"If that's not the definition of a pickup, I don't know what is," Kayla inserted.

But Miranda looked happier and that was all that Basilio was worried about. She smiled at him. "I'm glad to hear that."

"Be assured you are not one of many." She was, in fact, the only woman who could give his family what they so desperately needed: peace.

Miranda let out a small gasp, but the sound that came from her brother-in-law was far more cynical.

Basilio gave him a dry look. "How do you like venture capitalism? Different from digital security?"

"You meant to run into Randi!" Kayla exclaimed. "You wanted to meet Andreas. You know who he is."

Miranda's head jerked, and her beautiful gray eyes filled with hurt.

This was getting ridiculous. Basilio frowned at the sister. "While I applaud your concern for Miranda, please stop putting such negative thoughts into her head. I assure you, if I wanted to meet your husband to discuss a business venture, he would take my call."

Andreas narrowed his gaze. "Don't glower at my wife. She's just looking out for Randi."

"As I said, laudable, but unnecessary."

"What does he mean, Andreas? Do you know something about Basilio?" Kayla asked.

Andreas's jaw hardened, like he'd just realized who Basilio was. "Basilio Perez is the president of the worldwide real estate and hotel consortium known as Perez Holdings. He has fingers in more pies than Sebastian Hawk."

"You are?" Miranda asked, looking pale.

"I am. That does not change your desire to dine

with me, does it?" he teased, knowing it wouldn't. He'd never met a woman not drawn to his power and position.

She looked like she wasn't sure of her answer, though. "I'm not in your league."

"I'm not looking for a baseball team to dine with, just one quirky, charming woman and her very suspicious relatives." Not that they had nothing to worry about in her regard, but their concerns were in all the wrong directions.

While Basilio dated his fair share of women, he was by no means a womanizer. And he was not looking to use her for her family business connections.

"Oh, that's kind of sweet," Kayla said.

Miranda nodded. "It is."

Andreas was still watching Basilio with suspicion. However, after they ordered their food and the evening progressed, the other man thawed some. Basilio found himself actually enjoying conversation with the somewhat socially awkward Kayla, her very business-savvy husband and the unexpectedly sweet Miranda.

"So, are you here looking at an acquisition?" Andreas asked at one point.

Basilio put down his glass of very good scotch

after taking a sip. "That's not something I can discuss."

"Why not?" Miranda asked, pausing with the bite of steak she had been about to eat dangling on her fork.

"If word got out I was looking at a property, the sale price would increase immediately."

"Because you have deep pockets?" Miranda asked, sounding like she was trying to understand.

"Exactly." He was, in fact, looking at a property, a historic hotel that had closed down and would need extensive remodeling and updates before it could be opened again.

But the property was beautiful and the bones of the hotel were strong. He hadn't made a decision about the purchase yet, though.

"So, property acquisition is your thing?" Kayla asked.

"Sometimes." He had too much to do running Perez Holdings for him to be a full-time acquisitions manager. "I enjoy it."

"Then maybe you can help Randi find the property for our expansion house."

"Expansion house?" he asked, like he didn't have all the details in his report on the family back in his hotel suite.

"I run Kayla's for Kids." Miranda smiled, her tone saying how much satisfaction her job gave her. "It's a shelter for children and youth."

"Not their parents?"

Miranda's smile did not dim. "If their parents are around, we have services to help them, but our focus is the kids. The number of homeless teenagers and children in need of a safe place after school is greater than the facilities available to serve them."

"And you want to help these children?" Was she looking for absolution in service after what she'd done five years before?

"I do." Miranda's eyes darkened to molten silver. "Children deserve the best we can give them, but just as important, they are the beginning of change. If we give them hope for now, a chance to learn and grow, there's no way of knowing how much each child will touch and influence the world in their lifetime."

"So it starts with giving them a place to play games after school?"

"And experience art, a place to read a book in peace, a place to be safe." Her passion was damn near addictive.

Could he believe she was that committed to the

welfare of children and still be the woman willing to tear his own nephew's life apart with media interest?

"You are adding on another shelter, then?" he asked.

"Yes, where the rate of homeless teens is one of the highest." She named a western suburb of Portland. "But I don't expect you to help me find the building. I'm sure you're way too busy."

"On the contrary, I would be happy to help you." Doing so would give him the excuse he required to spend time with her.

"Really?" she asked, her lovely face covered in delight.

"Yes."

"That's great. I'm supposed to look at properties tomorrow."

"Send me a list of the properties and your requirements for the shelter. I'll vet them and see what else I can find for you."

"Seriously? You'd do that? I've got a Realtor working with me. She's going to donate her commission to the shelter, but doesn't seem to understand the concept of a budget and long-term running costs."

"Send me her name, as well, and I will make

sure she understands your requirements, or I will find a Realtor who will."

"Oh, I don't want you intimidating her. Like I said, she's generously donating her commission to the shelter."

"That donated commission could end up costing you quite a bit more in the long run."

"I tried to tell both Kayla and Randi this." Andreas gave both women a speaking look. "But they're convinced that anyone willing to donate their income is as committed to the best interests of the shelter as they are."

"Give me her name and I will make certain."

Miranda bit her lip. "I really don't want you scaring her."

"You think I would?"

"Um, just sitting at dinner with you is a little intimidating. Being under your scrutiny in a business setting?" Miranda gave an exaggerated shiver. "That would be downright frightening."

"And then some," Kayla said with a firm nod.

Andreas looked just a little horrified at his wife's honesty, but Basilio merely laughed, not offended in the least. He filed away the knowledge that Miranda was quite a bit more discerning than he'd given her credit for.

She might even recognize on some subconscious level that he was a danger to her. Unfortunately for her, she didn't understand just how ruthless he really was.

No man got to where he was in the business world without being an apex predator.

CHAPTER TWO

RANDI CAUGHT HER breath as Baz put his arm around her waist to walk to the piano bar.

He was so virile and strong. Rich and gorgeous.

An overwhelming example of the male species, and that was no exaggeration.

She was having a hard time understanding what he was doing with her. She wasn't hideous. Or embarrassingly awkward company, but that didn't mean she was the usual sort of date for a man like Basilio Perez.

Randi knew who and what she was. A usually shy, moderately pretty woman, who found the company of children easier to navigate than most single men.

She didn't date a lot, especially after the accident five years ago. Unable to deal with the media frenzy and social media ostracization, the man she'd thought she was going to marry had broken things off. Then Randi had been tricked into dating a reporter who wanted the inside scoop on the woman accused of destroying a family with her carelessness.

Each defection had devastated and demoralized her, the loss of friendships and even her university scholarship only adding to her sense of betrayal. She'd learned not to trust quickly or easily, not with new friends and particularly not with possible boyfriends.

She never allowed strange men to talk her into dinner and drinks.

But Baz wasn't exactly some random stranger. He was the president of a multibillion-dollar conglomerate. No way did he have a hidden agenda. Randi had nothing the man could want.

However, that didn't make this date any less bewildering, not to mention disturbing. The more time she spent with him, the more her attraction to him grew. She'd never felt anything as powerful. She *wanted* him. Seriously, deeply.

His arm around her waist was not helping her sense of self-control, either.

That simple point of contact ratcheting up the unexpected, unfamiliar and yet incredible sensations of desire coursing through her.

"So, um, do you come to Portland often?" She nearly winced at her gauche question. It sounded like she was fishing for the future and she was too smart to think they had one of those.

"This is my first time."

"Really? It's an amazing city that prides itself on being weird." She adored the eccentricity mixed with a good dose of cosmopolitan culture and had grown to love her new home in a very short amount of time.

"So I've been told."

"I just moved here a couple of months ago, but I wouldn't mind showing you some of the sights, if you like." Randi waited with cautious hope for Baz's answer to what was for her a very bold and unprecedented offer.

"I would like that." Dark eyes glinting with something like satisfaction, he smiled down at her. "Getting a feeling for the area is part of how I make decisions about whether or not to buy."

"So you *are* here looking for a property." She knew it.

But she did her best to ignore the tendril of hope unfurling inside her. If he bought a property, he'd come back. Wouldn't he?

"Perhaps" was all he said.

She laughed, finding something about his caginess endearing. "I'm not going to blab. Even if

I did, who could I tell that would impact you?" she teased. "I'm a social worker, not a real estate mogul."

His responding laughter sent shivers of sensation through her. "As you say."

"But you're still not going to tell me, are you?"

"No."

"You're a very cautious man."

"I would not be where I am if I were not."

"Walking down the street with a woman you just met hours ago?" She made no effort to hide the laughter in her voice, because really? If she was acting impulsively, so was he.

He stopped and pulled her around to face him, their bodies inches apart, his attention intent and on her only. "You enjoy your own humor, don't you?"

"Someone should."

He wasn't smiling exactly, but humor gleamed in his espresso-brown gaze. "You are not as shy as you appear at first."

"I feel comfortable with you." Which was really dangerous, but she also found him super-attractive. Could attraction undermine common sense completely? She'd never thought so, but she was adjusting her thinking on that issue fast.

"That is good to know."

"I think so, too." Her words trailed off as his head lowered toward hers. She stared up into his dark gaze; her lips parted of their own accord. "Are you going to kiss me?"

His answer was his mouth pressing to hers.

Sensation exploded inside Randi. Zings of electric current coursed through her body, radiating outward from where their lips touched and sending goose bumps in waves over her skin. Need like she had never known throbbed in her core, making her press her thighs together in instinctive effort to alleviate it. It didn't work, of course.

She ached for way more than a simple kiss.

Though there was nothing *simple* about the way Baz's lips *owned* hers, giving no quarter, demanding response or submission, with no option for backing off.

At least as far as her body's response would allow.

Though his hands were on her upper arms, Baz did not actively hold her in place with anything but the press of his lips. Randi responded on a primal, visceral level that would not allow her to hold back, bringing forth sensations she'd read about, but never actually experienced.

Overwhelming passion. Gut-level desire that burned hotter than the California wildfires in the summer. Her nipples beaded with near-painful intensity; her most intimate flesh pulsed with a need for touch; her lips softened and molded to his with hungry ardency.

Randi reveled in every single unfamiliar sensation, responding to the kiss in a way that a public display on the busy sidewalk did not warrant, her own lack of control acting as an irresistible aphrodisiac.

She could no more help giving him kiss for kiss than she could stop breathing.

Breathing might even be less necessary.

Randi curled her fingers around the lapels of Baz's suit jacket, pulling his body closer to hers. Only then did warm, masculine arms come around her, holding her tight now, his hands pressed tightly to her back and just at the top of her buttocks.

The kiss morphed into something more than possession. It became two people equally intent, equally impassioned, equally lost to their desires.

There could be no doubt, until Baz pulled his head back.

At least his breathing was ragged like hers, his expression pained. "We've got to stop. On a public sidewalk is not the place for this."

Randi didn't care. This was something new for

her. Something craved. Something *needed*. Refusing to give up the amazing sensations his kiss caused, she rose on her tiptoes, seeking his mouth again, only realizing as his lips cut them off that the needy little sounds she heard were coming from her.

And she did not care. There could be no embarrassment in this level of yearning.

He groaned, the deep, masculine sound traveling through her body, leaving devastation in its wake. Baz invaded her mouth with his tongue. It was not finessed; the demand of his tongue sliding against hers had no lead in, no buildup to the increased intimacy, and again… Randi *did not care.*

She opened wider for him, melting under the demanding forays. Her tongue tangled with his, taking in his taste, unlike any other taste, pure sex, pure man. Randi kissed him back, letting him feel the unfamiliar and overwhelming passion exploding inside her.

He made a deep sound in his throat, all male want, but then he did the unthinkable. Again.

His hands landing on her shoulders to push her away at the same time as he broke the connection between their mouths for the second time was not only not welcome, it was also torture. Didn't he understand? She needed his lips, his tongue, his arms tight around her.

She could not suppress the sound of keen disappointment, or control her involuntary move back toward him.

But Baz was made of sterner stuff than she was, apparently, because he held her firmly away. "No, Miranda. Not here. We have put on enough of an entertainment for others."

She looked around and saw that they did indeed have an audience, several smiles and thumbs-ups directed her way. Only in Portland.

Blushing to the roots of her hair, Randi allowed herself to be set away from the source of her temptation. "I guess we should go into the piano bar, huh?"

Baz inclined his head. "If that is what you wish."

"I…" What was he saying? Was he ready for the evening to be over?

"Or we could go into the hotel and get a room?" he suggested.

She'd never done that, not once. Randi had not only never had a one-off with a man she'd just met, she'd also never rented a hotel room with a man for the sole purpose of having sex. The illicit nature of the idea was way too alluring.

And that worried her. Where was her deeply in-grained sense of self-preservation?

She asked the only thing her mind could conjure without giving away just how much she wanted to do exactly as he suggested. "Don't you have a room already?"

His shrug was dismissive. "An executive pent-house condo, but getting there would require wait-ing to have my car brought around by the valet. Besides, I can't travel alone. If I'm in my pent-house, my staff can find me even if I turn off my phone."

She couldn't imagine that kind of pressure, the knowledge that privacy and alone time were little more than an illusion. Even so.

"You're saying you want me so much you want to get a room, right here at the Heathman, so we can..." She couldn't make herself spell it out.

"Pick up where that kiss left off, yes."

"Oh."

"Oh?"

"I mean, yes, I'd like that." *What was she say-ing?* Was she agreeing to a hookup in a hotel room with a man she'd only met hours ago?

And if she was, why wasn't she more freaked out about the idea?

Randi was barely a nonvirgin, having had sex exactly twice. Neither of which had turned out well for her. She and her almost fiancé had gotten intimate just before the accident and subsequent media storm. The reporter had gotten Randi into bed after a few weeks of dating and pretending to be someone else, only to walk away the next morning with his exclusive.

But Baz was not some jerk with a hidden agenda who would break her heart after using her body. It might only be one night; their mutual passion might be a temporary aberration, but at least she wasn't worried about the aftermath.

Randi was tired of living in the bubble of loneliness that had surrounded her for the past five years.

Whatever happened tomorrow, tonight she got what she just knew was going to be amazing sex, with the most magnetic man she'd ever spoken to, much less kissed.

Baz looked down at her, his dark-chocolate gaze filled with desire. "Well?"

An atavistic chill ran down her spine. This man was a primal alpha and she wanted to meet him passion for passion. "Yes."

"Yes to the hotel room?"

She nodded.

"I need the word, *mi hermosa*. There can be no doubt."

"Yes."

His smile was killer. *"Muy bien. Vente mi, cariña."* He took her hand and set a fast pace for the main entrance to the hotel.

So, he lost his English when he was turned on. Randi liked knowing she could affect him so strongly. And she liked the endearments, too. Even if it was only a one-night stand, what woman didn't want to be called beautiful and darling? Though *beautiful* might be stretching it, she wasn't about to tell him so. Let the man look at her through the filter of lust-filled glasses.

She hadn't been into the main lobby of the Heathman in years, its nearly hundred-year-old beauty as pristine as when it had first been built in the nineteen-twenties. Both luxurious and gorgeous, with its decorative, rich wood walls and pillars, two-story-high ceiling and elegant decor, the cavernous room intended for greeting guests was nothing short of awe-inspiring. Baz, international business mogul, led her to the desk and had no trouble procuring a room, despite his lack of reservations. The fact he was happy to take the

Grand Suite for the night probably had something to do with that.

Randi couldn't help gasping when she heard the clerk tell Baz how much one night would be. She could pay the rent on her small apartment for two months with what he was willing to pay to have the convenience of a hotel room right that minute.

With original art on the walls—art rarely seen outside a museum, no less—the suite's full-size living room and dining area decorated in pure modern elegance was separated from the bedroom by a spacious foyer, making the suite bigger than her apartment and way more lavish.

"Stop looking at the furniture. I want your eyes on me," Baz instructed as he pulled her into his arms.

"But this place is incredible," she teased, having no problem following his demands.

Even the opulent suite couldn't hold a candle to the man pulling her close into his body.

Baz's expression turned thoughtful. "You like it? The clerk said it was booked for tomorrow, but I could probably persuade them to accommodate us."

Of course the billionaire thought so, despite the

fact it was probably some kind of celebrity coming in to stay.

"No. I… It's just… This place is bigger than my apartment!"

His smile was indulgent. "And would you rather explore it, or me?"

That fast, the desire buzzing along her nerve endings went critical. "You."

"Then let us go to the bedroom."

And without warning, she was suddenly in his arms, being carried like a princess into a bedroom fit for royalty. He set her down and ripped the extra pillows from the bed, tossing them onto the floor, before flinging back the duvet.

Then he turned to her. "I think we are both overdressed for what is about to happen."

Her mouth gone instantly dry, she nodded.

He slipped off his tailored suit jacket and hung it carelessly on an armchair, before toeing off his shoes so he could slip his trousers off and do the same with them. His legs were pillars of muscle; his olive skin sprinkled with dark, masculine hair. He kicked off his socks without looking away from her, no evidence of even the slightest discomfort in his near nudity.

Paralyzed with want and no small dose of insecurity she'd rather pretend she never felt, Randi just watched the Spanish business shark strip.

"You are not going to join me?" he asked, his tone teasing, no doubt there that she wanted what he so clearly did.

The power tie went next, and then the buttons on his shirt before Baz shrugged it off to lay it over his other clothes on the chair, putting acres of golden olive skin on display.

She sucked in air as his muscular, defined torso and chest came into view. "I think your abs have abs. What do you do, like a million sit-ups a day or something?"

"My exercise routine is what you want to talk about?" he demanded, humor lacing his voice, but oh, his eyes.

They burned with everything she felt.

Truthfully? She didn't want to talk at all. Randi wanted to touch, crossing the few feet of carpet separating them to do just that.

While the tent in his snug, black, silk-knit boxers called to her, she reached up to brush her hands through the black hair on his chest. "So soft."

"You expected something else?"

"I've never been with a man with chest hair before," she admitted.

"I do not want to hear about other men."

His words thrilled her, but she wasn't so far gone she was going to let him see that. "So possessive for a one-night stand."

"You believe I will have all I want of you in a single night?" he asked with disbelief. "Not a chance."

The breath in her lungs whooshed out. "Good to know," she choked out.

His hands were on the hem of her gray knit dress, the smocking over her chest that she'd always considered cute and comfortable, now confining against sensitized flesh and peaked nipples. He pulled the dress up and over her head without another word and she let him, the cuffs on the three-quarter-length sleeves catching for a breathless second on her hands, leaving her blinded by fabric and vulnerable before him.

"Bella," he husked out as the dress finally disappeared, giving her a renewed view of Baz. Heated espresso eyes burned her with their intensity as his gaze ate her up. "You are a surprise."

Again with the beautiful. Randi had reason to be glad she'd learned Spanish in order to communicate with the children whom she assumed would come through her office at social services for which it was their first language.

Only belatedly did she realize what exactly had him surprised, and apparently mesmerized. "My sister likes shopping at the lingerie store."

"And she takes you with her?" he asked as he made no effort to hide his fascination with her breasts covered by a sheer lift bra and the matching panties that allowed him to see the soft brown curls at the apex of her thighs, the fabric a pearlescent gossamer.

Under the perfectly opaque fabric of her dress, she could wear whatever sexy underwear she liked and never considered someone else seeing them. "They remind me I'm a sexual being."

A reminder she had needed very badly before tonight.

"I assure you, no one else could forget."

"Right." She didn't have her sister's generous curves, Randi's own body as subtle in its femininity as she was shy.

"You doubt me?" He indicated the rampant erection barely contained by his boxers. "You think I do this kind of thing with every woman I meet?"

Another blush heated her skin, but desire made

her even hotter. "No, I don't doubt you want me. I want you, too."

"Then let's get your boots off and you into bed."

She couldn't feel awkward standing there in her brown, nearly flat-heeled boots that reached her knees, and nothing else besides the diaphanous underwear. Not with the approval glowing in his dark gaze.

"You like this look?" she couldn't help teasing with a cant to her hips.

"Very much, but I believe you will be more comfortable without footwear."

She nodded. Even in her current state, she'd feel all kinds of wrong climbing onto the luxurious bed with her shoes on.

They made quick work of her boots and then she was on her back, on the bed.

Baz pulled off her panties, his gaze fixed firmly on the triangle of curls hiding her most sensitive flesh. "I love the sexy lingerie, but full access is even more exciting."

Feeling embarrassed for the first time, she put her hand over herself. "I used to wax."

"I prefer this. Did you know if I touch you carefully, like so..." He gently pulled her hand away before his fingertips barely brushed over the tips of her private curls. "You will feel it deep inside."

She couldn't help the arch upward, or the gasp of pleasure as his caress made truth out of his words. Really? Her *hair* was an erogenous zone, and quite an effective one. Desire ran rampant through her blood, every nerve ending on high alert for the barest touch from him.

"You are beautiful here." No question, from where he was looking and the brush of his fingers, what he was talking about.

"That…you…" She wanted to deny the words, deny that he could find her most intimate place *beautiful*. "That's for touching, not looking."

He got off the bed, stripped off his boxers and indicated his very hard, very big—at least in her experience—and very obvious erection. "You do not get turned on seeing my sex?"

Why was he asking her this? "You're awfully blunt." But she couldn't move her gaze away from tumescent flesh and knew deep in her heart that seeing it soft would be no less arousing.

His expression dared her to deny his words.

She wasn't a liar. "Yes, seeing you excites me. A lot." But she hadn't realized it would, hadn't thought of herself as a visual person when it came to sex.

"And looking at you, the very part of yourself you hold most private, inflames me." His accent had thickened, lending a warm Latin lilt to his words.

He rejoined her on the bed, straddling her thighs, his erection pressed against her sensitized mound.

He ran a finger along the bit of exposed breast above the top of her bra. *"Muy guapa."*

"I'm..." More compliments to her body. How was she supposed to take them?

The way Baz was with her, his touches and words, was so outside her experience in the bedroom—what little there was of it.

Randi gasped as he cupped both her breasts with his hands, rubbing expertly against her already hard and tight nipples through the silky fabric. "Glad. I'm glad."

"Good to know." His expression was all approval. "You are so responsive."

"I never have been."

His eyes narrowed as if he was thinking, his head cocked a little. "You aren't very experienced, are you?"

"You told me you didn't want to hear about other men."

"The lack thereof in your past is an unexpected turn-on."

"It is?" she gasped out as his ministrations to her breasts sent sensation zinging straight to the core of her.

"Yes."

"Unexpected?"

"As a rule, I stay away from women lacking in experience."

He wanted lovers who could keep up with him and maybe knew the score. Right? She understood that. And was doing her best to keep that score in mind, no matter how devastating his touch.

A billionaire Spanish businessman wasn't going to keep a social worker from her family background, even if he *did* want more than one night. She did, too, so that was okay. Right?

She wasn't going to fall in love with this sexy man.

She wasn't.

"But not me," she confirmed.

"No. Not you. You, I want."

"I want you, too."

He leaned down and kissed her then, his tongue

demanding entrance almost immediately. She gave it to him, reveling in how he took control of her body and the kiss. She'd never wanted to give herself this way, to let a man touch her like she was *his*.

Randi's characteristic cling to independence and self-control, no matter the situation, was conspicuously absent, though.

His hands were all over her body, touching spots she had no idea could be erogenous, but which had her repeatedly arching up off the bed, seeking more. She wanted to touch him, too, but somehow every time she went to caress him, she lost her focus and her hands ended up resting against his chest, kneading like a cat with her short nails.

He seemed to like that, groaning against her lips, moving his body to spread her legs and press his erection firmly against her most tender flesh. Randi went taut with pleasure as he somehow managed to maneuver his erection against her clitoris in mock coupling, thrusting against her and stimulating her so well she cried out with the joy of it.

Randi gasped out her pleasure at the amazing feeling. "Baz! Oh…" It was too good, too much, her body racking with shudders of ecstasy.

"You are so deliciously responsive, Miranda."
His voice deep with approval and husky desire,
Baz continued to thrust against her, his big hands
inciting her pleasure with incredible knowledge of
the female body and what would feel good.

She tossed her head on the fluffy pillows, feeling like she needed something more, but unwilling
to change what was already giving her so much
marvelous sensation. "You're really good at this."

"This?" he teased, gently rolling her nipples between thumb and forefinger.

Oh, wow. That was… It was… Even her inner
monologue could not come up with the right ad-
jectives. She'd never before realized the direct line
between the turgid peaks and her feminine sex.
Sure, it felt good to be touched there, but never
like lightning was striking through her body.

"Yes, that and all of it."

"It is easy to give pleasure when it is so well received."

"Are you saying I'm easy?" she gasped out, teasing and not.

She'd never found it so simple to give in, to
allow a man so close so fast. This whole confla-
gration between their bodies was entirely outside
her experience.

Sex was not all that.

Only now it was. Now it was everything. Necessary.

"I would never be so crass."

That was not a denial. She met his gaze earnestly. "I'm not, you know."

"Not?"

"Easy. I don't *do* one-night stands."

"Good, but fair warning—I have no intention of stopping at one night with you."

He wasn't offering anything long-term. How could he? He lived in Spain. She lived in Portland. He was a powerful billionaire. A social worker turned shelter manager had no place in his glittery life, but for now? She did.

She fit in this ridiculously expensive bed he'd bought for the night.

Her body fit under his. Her lips fit perfectly against his.

His mouth owned hers and she let it. Knowing this was temporary, but not a single night, gave her the confidence to let go in a way she had not before, and probably wouldn't again, with anyone else.

She responded to his kiss, parting her lips, inviting his tongue inside, letting hers explore his mouth, shivering with feeling as the kiss morphed into something crazy passionate. Her body melted into the bed under him, accommodating his hard planes with every cell.

He lifted up enough to pull her toward him so he could remove that last piece of clothing she was wearing, her bra.

When he let her settle back against the pillows, Randi reached down between them and grasped his erection, the heated, satiny skin warming her palm.

He thrust up into her fist. *"Sí! Que es tan bueno."*

It *was* good. All of it. Randi loved knowing she could elicit such a pleasurable response, that her touch impacted him as surely as his touch made Randi lose her mind.

"I want this inside me." She squeezed the hard column of flesh once…twice, again.

Baz let out a guttural sound that sent response arcing through Randi. He reared back but didn't pull his sex from her hand, though she got the sense that was his initial intent. "Let me get a condom."

"You just carry them around with you?"

"I do, in fact, always have one in my wallet." He shrugged. "I am a man."

"We're going to need more." No way was a single time going to be enough tonight. Not for such a sexually ardent lover.

"I'll take care of that later." His smile was all predatory male.

CHAPTER THREE

RANDI NODDED, HER words lost for a moment in the pleasure of their bodies together.

Long moments passed in another incendiary kiss, his sex pressing into her hand, her own aching with the need to be filled. When he finally broke the kiss to get up, she made a mewing sound she'd never heard out of her own throat before.

He stood with quick, efficient movements, and moved to the chair on which his trousers lay with a few long, rapid strides. Seconds later he was back beside her, the condom packet in his hand. "Do you want to put it on me?"

In answer, Randi eagerly reached for the foil square. Baz dropped it into her hand and she tore it open, pulling out the small bit of latex. She pressed the circle of latex against the head of his penis, thrilling to the moment of anticipation this particular act elicited. She rolled it down his length, an intentional caress with more enjoyment than experience, hoping to make the act erotic for both of them.

He didn't seem to mind her fumbling attempts at covering him. He was, in fact, moaning and staring at her with clear sexual approval.

Once she got the condom on, he pushed her onto her back, but instead of immediately moving between her thighs, as she expected, he reached down to touch her, his fingers deftly caressing her slick folds.

"Oh, goodness! This is…that is…" Exactly what she needed, making her incoherent with sensation, senseless words of pleasure tumbling from her lips.

He seemed to have no problem deciphering her babbling, touching exactly where she needed. Sliding his fingers over her clitoris, gently circling, pushing gently at intervals, he caressed her with just the right pressure before slipping one, then two inside her, preparing her for what was to come.

She could no more stop her body surging toward his touch than reach out with her own hands, seeking the lodestone of his body. Anything to help her maintain sanity in this maelstrom of emotion and sensation, where by rights no emotion should be.

They did not know each other. It should be pure physicality, but her heart was beating a strange, desperate tattoo of feeling she had no desire to acknowledge.

Baz crooked his fingers inside her and pressed upward. Jolts of intense ecstasy radiated out from that heretofore unexplored cluster of nerves inside her. She'd heard about the G-spot, but thought it was a myth. Oh, glorious elation, it wasn't!

Rapture spiraled inside Randi, drawing her body tight with impending orgasm, but Baz was careful not to take her over the edge.

Darn it!

She tried to move her body, to take herself over that precipice. "Please, Baz. Please!"

"You will come with me inside you," he proclaimed, even as he *finally* shifted between her legs to press his engorged sex against the slick and swollen opening to her body.

"I've never come from that," she warned him, though just the feeling of him so close to penetrating her was setting off all sorts of fireworks inside her. Not that she had loads of experiences to go by anyway, but neither time had made her believe she was one of those women who could.

"Let us see what we can do about that." Challenge gleamed in his espresso-brown eyes.

A shiver of anticipation—or was that trepidation?—rolled through her. "Just do me," she implored, not caring if she climaxed in that moment.

She was empty. She needed to be filled and Baz Perez with his big, hard sex would succeed where she knew others had failed. Giving her pleasure and a sense of completion, even if she didn't actually come from it.

But Baz, she learned quickly, did not dismiss a challenge. He attacked it with skill, patience and purpose.

He made love to her as no other guy had done, driving the pleasure inside her body higher and higher with each expert thrust, every swivel of his hips that managed to stimulate her clitoris in ways she'd thought impossible during copulation. Finally, he reached down and brushed over that swollen nub with his thumb, at first pressing in and then circling, then pressing in again, then circling, and Randi lost what sense she'd maintained.

The euphoria building inside her detonated, the roman candle of ecstasy exploding with a shower of sparks throughout her body. Her womb contracted, her muscles convulsed and her heart nearly seized from the glorious power of it. She cried out as her vaginal walls tightened around his hard sex in spasms of pure bliss.

"That's right," he praised, his body taut with unfulfilled desire. "You are so beautiful in your excitement."

The words registered only peripherally as her body shuddered with a surfeit of pleasure. "Baz…"

She couldn't say anything more than his name, couldn't form a coherent thought, could only arch against him, prolonging the overwhelming sensation. He resumed movement, his lunges growing more powerful with each surge forward of his pelvis, strong thrusts inside her causing aftershocks of ecstasy nearly as intense as her initial orgasm.

"*Sí, hermosa, sí!* You are so perfect inside. Tight, hot, wet."

Oh, man, did men really talk like that in bed?

"You hold me like a warm, slick fist."

Clearly, they did.

And those words intensified the residual waves of excitement. "Baz, oh, Baz!"

With a final lunge forward, he went rigid above her and then gave a low, guttural shout, filling the condom with his hot spend, his face fixed in a rictus of ultimate pleasure.

Randi reached up with arms like noodles to clasp his shoulders, needing even more connection than the ultimate joining of their bodies. "I… you…"

He kissed her, cutting off whatever she'd been about to say. She kissed him back, reveling in the press of soft lips against soft lips while he was still inside her.

No other moment in her life had been so perfect.

Later, after he'd taken care of the condom and cleaned up in the en suite, Baz ran a bath in the jetted tub.

Randi lounged in the bed, feeling decadent surrounded by luxury linens and the sound of running water. She heard him on the phone, too, but couldn't make out his words.

When he returned to the bedroom, she asked if he had to leave.

He leaned against the doorjamb, gloriously naked, unashamed by what others might consider vulnerability. "Why would you think that?"

"You were on the phone." For men like him and Andreas, a phone call, whatever the time, often precipitated the need for some kind of action on their part.

Billionaires were busy people, or so she'd learned since her sister and Kayla's new husband came into Randi's life.

"I called housekeeping and asked for a box of condoms to be delivered. Then I called room service and ordered champagne and strawberries." Baz let his lips tilt in an enigmatic half smile. "It seemed appropriate."

Who ordered condoms to their room? "Lavish."

"And do you not deserve lavish?" he asked in what should have been a tease, but something in his gaze probed hers with serious intent.

"It's not my norm, that's for sure." She wasn't the one with a super-rich husband catering to her every need.

That was her sister, and Randi loved the way Andreas took such pains to care for Kayla, but Randi refused to let her brother-in-law subsidize *her* living expenses, so she made do on what she considered a generous salary from the shelter. Though it hardly stretched to the kind of luxury Baz seemed to take for granted.

He shifted away from the door, his big body moving with surprising elegance, despite his lack of clothing. "I will enjoy spoiling you."

And she would probably enjoy being spoiled.

Too much. Too easy to get used to the attention, but as long as she never forgot it was temporary, she might actually survive with her heart intact.

"You're not like any other man I know." She sat up. Letting the bedclothes fall away from her body, she reminded herself that he'd already seen everything she might try to hide and had seemed to like it very much.

His gaze ran over her with more heat than she would expect so soon after what they'd just finished. "Men like me are a rare breed."

"You so are."

His smile was lethal as he leaned down to pull her from the bed. "Come on. I have a mind to share a *lavish* bath with you."

"A bath is a bath."

Minutes later as she sat in the steaming, scented bathtub, water made ultra-soft with oils, a plate of chocolate-dipped strawberries within reach, two glasses of champagne perched on the tub's lip, Randi had reason to retract her own statement.

"Okay, this is definitely sumptuous."

"You think?" Baz had donned the complimentary robe to receive both the delivery from housekeeping and room service.

"I do, yes."

He dropped the robe and stepped toward her, once again magnificently naked. "You look like a nymph in that swirling water."

"Not hardly." Randi had a mirror, and sea nymph, she was not.

"Do not ruin my fantasy with your sense of the prosaic."

"I would not have considered you a fantasy kind of guy."

"We all have dreams."

"I suppose."

"Don't you have dreams, aspirations, desires?"

"I learned five years ago that life doesn't dole out the fulfillment of dreams equally to everybody." After all, she'd been on the cusp of engagement with her boyfriend, enrolled at her top choice university and surrounded by friends and a family who loved her. She'd come to terms with having a wholly narcissistic mom with tendencies toward violence when thwarted, and Randi had been, for a time, really happy.

His attention sharpened, his expression assessing. "What happened five years ago?"

"My world imploded."

"You cannot make such a statement and not explain."

She shook her head. "Some things are too painful for the consumption of strangers."

"Are we still strangers?" His expression turned carnal. "I would say we have enjoyed some very intimate moments."

"We've been intimate with our *bodies*," she emphasized. "Emotions and memories are another thing entirely." A man with his experience couldn't believe anything else, could he?

Baz climbed into the hot water with her, muscular limbs sliding against hers, accentuating the lack of barrier between them. Renewed desire sent a flush over her body, more acute than that brought on by the hot water.

His hand traveled up Randi's leg from her ankle, stopping at the top of her inner thigh. "Let's get a little more physically intimate, then, shall we?"

"Yes." Relief that he was not pushing for answers about something she hadn't meant to mention mixed with sensual delight as his hand moved against her inner thigh.

His fingertips rubbed against her most intimate flesh, making her languid with need.

He tugged her unresisting body closer. "Come here, *mi hermosa*."

She let herself be pulled into him and maneuvered so she was facing away from him, leaning against the bulging muscles of his body. There was something so sexy about being in his arms in the water, her back to him, his hands on her. The message going to her sexual brain was that he was focused on her pleasure. And her pleasure alone.

Maybe she should feel bad, should do something to balance the focus, but she didn't. This whole night, so far, felt too good, too different from anything she'd ever known.

His hands moved up her body, caressing her hips, her torso and finally settling to cup her breasts, touching already sensitized nipples, sending thrills of bliss through her.

Lips brushed behind her ear. "You are addictive, *cariña*."

"The way you make me feel could easily become a necessary habit." And wasn't that terrifying? Because he *wasn't* sticking around.

No way could he.

Not Mr. Spanish Billionaire Businessman.

"Good to hear." He nibbled against her neck, sending shivers throughout her body.

"You think so?" Was he really blind to how bad that could be for her?

"Don't you?" he asked against her skin, before

tugging ever so gently on her earlobe with his teeth.

She convulsed with a new set of shivers. "Not so much, no."

His laugh was unexpected, husky and warm. "You are very refreshing, Miranda."

"I guess *that* is a good thing."

He made a noncommittal sound. Maybe he'd miss refreshing. Maybe addictive was just as bad for his long-term peace of mind as hers.

One of his hands left her breast, and seconds later, a chocolate-dipped strawberry pressed against her lips. "Take a bite." The words whispered against her ear, making the prosaic instruction all sensual and sexy.

Randi opened her mouth and let the dark chocolate and strawberry flavors burst on her tongue as she did what he told her to. She ate with decadent delight, taking a sip of her champagne after finishing the strawberry. All the while Baz continued to caress her entire body with tender stimulation, one hand touching her with more effect than should be possible.

She plucked a strawberry from the plate, then reached back to offer it to him. Baz took a bite, letting his tongue flick out to taste her fingers, sending more pleasure jolting through her. As she fed him the rest of the fruit, he continued to lave her fingers, pulling one into his mouth and sucking on the digit with sensual mastery.

"That feels good," she panted, her words coming out on separate little gasps of air. "It shouldn't feel so good."

"You think not?" he asked after releasing her finger from his mouth.

"I… No…it's not something…"

"You are so experienced, then," he gently mocked.

She had no thought to lie. "No, I'm not in your league." Her heart rate sped up as his fingers rubbed over her clitoris in the slippery water. "I think we both know that."

"We've already discussed this."

"And you pretended ignorance to what I meant, but be real. You're a player."

"I am not." He sounded affronted. "In fact, I never have more than one sex partner at a time."

"Serial monogamy." She'd heard the term before, but never known someone it *fit*.

"If you like."

"And right now, I'm it?" she asked with disbelief, even as her body warned her that logical reasoning was going to shut down soon in the face of abject ecstasy.

"*Sí.*"

"No woman back in Spain?"

"None."

"I'm not seeing anyone, either."

"That is good to know."

Something in her instincts told her he was the type of man who would have checked before bedding her the first time. Why hadn't he? Had he been as lost to physical sensation as she?

Her thoughts scattered as his touch changed and the orgasm she'd thought was well off was suddenly right *there*. Spasms of pleasure rolled through her as he continued to stimulate her to the point just short of pain.

She grabbed his wrist, holding it tight. "Too much!"

He let his fingers slide away, wrapping her in a tight embrace she realized she needed desperately to keep her connected to reality. She'd never climaxed twice in one night and she had the distinct feeling they weren't done yet.

As her body eventually settled, Randi's breaths returned to normal and her heart scaled back from a beat that felt like it was coming out of her

chest, she became aware of the hard length pressing against her back. An erection she had every
intention of doing something about.

She turned in his arms, letting herself rub
against him before coming to rest with her arms
crossed on his sculpted chest. Satiated and le-
thargic, she still smiled up at him with invitation.
"You're still hard."

"I like a little self-denial."

"Why?"

"It makes the eventual climax all the stronger."

She stared at him. "I think I don't even know as
much about sex as I thought I did."

"You know what you need to." His return gaze
was filled with heat and maybe approval.

Did she? So far she'd been a very passive partner, and that didn't cut it for Randi. She might not
be as experienced as he was; she might not have
even realized some people did that thing with putting off their pleasure to make it stronger later, but
she was not a selfish lover.

"I believe I do," she agreed. "Will you sit on the
edge of the tub?"

"Why?"

"Because I want to taste you."

His jaw hardened at her words, the muscles in

his neck straining as he swallowed, his gaze going molten with lust.

Right. He liked the idea.

If there'd been any doubts, the swiftness with which he moved to a sitting position, with his legs the only thing in the water, settled them.

Randi pressed his legs apart and moved to kneel between them, her own womb contracting in re-membered pleasure at the sight of his tumescent flesh.

Reaching out, she took him in her hand, her fingertips not quite touching. "You're thick," she murmured huskily.

"I'm extremely turned on. Touch me like that and you'll make me come."

"That's the idea." Before he could retort, she dropped her head forward and took the tip of his erection in her mouth.

He muttered an imprecation, which she took as approval.

Licking him, she took in his taste, all male and exactly what she craved, the pearls of pre-ejacu-late almost sweet. Randi suckled his tip while run-ning her hand up and down his length, loving the feel of his silky uncircumcised flesh moving over his hard column of flesh. Muttering something in Spanish she did not recognize so assumed was blue language, he settled one of his hands on her head. He did not press for her to take more of his big sex into her mouth, but his hand completed the circle of their connection.

If she didn't watch herself, she'd nuzzle into the hold, exposing more than she wanted.

His hand in her hair excited her, but she wasn't getting sidetracked from her final goal of bringing him the ultimate pleasure. She caressed his balls with the hand not around his penis, very careful not to press too hard on fragile skin, reveling in the spate of Spanish curses that touch elicited.

He gave a hoarse cry. "Yes, keep touching me, *mi hermosa. Que es tan bueno.*"

She didn't need words telling her how good it was, not with his reaction, but she enjoyed the fervent Spanish anyway. She would have smiled if her mouth wasn't full of him, her heart warmed at his approval. Doing her best to take as much as she could of him into her mouth, Randi stretched her lips wide, pressing forward of her own volition, very mindful of her teeth. She'd no desire to cause even the slightest pain to her temporary lover.

She didn't know how long she was lost in pleasuring him, but suddenly he was pulling her head away with the warning, "I'm coming. *Diablo, sí, ya voy.*"

He wrapped his hand around hers, guiding her to take a tighter grip on his column of flesh and increase her pace on the up and downward strokes. There was something really sexy about having his hand wrapped around hers, controlling his pleasure even as *she* gave it to him. Then he was shouting as he climaxed in her hand, barely missing her head with jets of his spend.

"You definitely have all the experience you need." Baz's voice, warm with approval and deep with sexual satisfaction, washed over her after he had regained control of his breathing.

Randi felt utter satisfaction that she'd brought him to this place.

Basilio woke with one arm under the head of his bed partner and the other wrapped snugly around her waist, barely stifling the instinctive curse the situation warranted.

He did not cuddle. Not even with lovers of what was for him long duration. Yet he'd spent the entire night either having sex with the woman in his arms, or holding her. They'd coupled twice more after her inexpert, but mind-shattering, blow job the night before.

He was the one that was supposed to be seducing her, bringing Miranda Smith, née Weber, around to his way of thinking in regard to doing that exposé interview. However, he'd been seduced himself by her innocent sensuality, her sexual candor, her enthusiasm for life and her understated beauty.

There was something about the sweet twenty-four-year-old that got under Basilio's skin.

He didn't give the emotion a sentimental name. It was just another aspect of sex he had not yet experienced. Basilio had promised himself at a tender age, he would never fall into the disastrous morass that romantic love and its companion emotions caused.

He'd seen the effect on his father of following that path, had felt those effects in his own young life as stepmothers changed too frequently for stability.

Nevertheless, he had a difficult time reconciling the woman in whose body he found such satisfying pleasure with the hard-hearted bitch that wanted to tear apart his family's peace.

While that did not change his plans to seduce her into agreeing to cancel the interview, it did have him wondering if there was an aspect to what happened five years ago that Basilio did not understand, or know about.

He needed to get her to talk about the past and why she thought going on television would help her own cause when he could only see heartbreak ahead for her. She'd done something many would find unforgivable. In a moment of inattention, she'd hit a child with her car. And while the consequences could have been worse, they'd been bad enough.

His phone buzzed, interrupting his thoughts, and Basilio carefully eased himself away from Miranda, her sleep so sound, she didn't so much as stir. He tucked the blankets around her, not wanting a draft to disturb her slumber.

She made a soft sound and snuggled into her pillow.

He allowed himself a smile of pure male satisfaction. He'd worn her out and he liked knowing it. Some might call him a throwback for his attitude, but he didn't really care.

He was who he was. And in other circumstances, Miranda Smith would be his ideal bed partner.

He grabbed his phone and swiped just before it went to voice mail. "Wait a moment," he instructed his brother while moving into the living room of the spacious suite.

"Baz?" his brother demanded impatiently, without waiting as Basilio had asked. "It's Carl."

"Sí." His phone had already told him as much.

"Have you talked to her yet?"

"I met her. I have not broached the subject of the interview."

"Why not?" his brother demanded, his tone caustic. "We're running out of time."

"There is still more than two weeks until she's scheduled to go on air."

"You need to take care of this now. We can't wait until the last minute." Carl could certainly be strident, but he failed to understand the dynamic of the situation.

"You asked for my help. You will take it as I offer it," Basilio informed his brother.

"Baz, have you forgotten who the younger brother is here?"

"Have you forgotten that you already managed to instigate a restraining order?" If his *older* brother hadn't screwed up, Carl wouldn't need Basilio's help.

"It was a misunderstanding."

"That resulted in legal action. It must have been a rather large misconception."

His brother huffed. "Look, just get her to agree. Tiffany can't take any more from this tragedy."

"Why wasn't there legal action taken at the time? Miranda was guilty of negligence in her driving at the very least."

"I don't know. That was a decision the DA made. Maybe it had something to do with her connections."

That did not ring true, and his brother should know it. "She has only recently discovered she's related to the wife of Andreas Kostas."

"Like I said, I don't know." But something about his brother's words did not have the feel of veracity.

"What about civil action? If you had sued her, she wouldn't be doing this supposed tell-all now, would she?" His brother's lawyers would have made sure part of the restitution would have been no publicity or book deals based on the tragedy Basilio's nephew had suffered.

"We were too distraught at the time. Now it is too late."

Basilio was pretty sure both of those claims were lies. So what was the real reason his brother had refused to take civil action against Miranda Smith?

Perhaps this was something Basilio needed to look further into. He'd never considered that there were extenuating circumstances to his nephew ending up in the hospital in a coma for two weeks, then needing to learn all over again how to speak. Even now he could not imagine what they could be, but one thing was certain.

Carl's attitude was off for the injured party.

Basilio acknowledged his cynicism could have something to do with the fact that he'd never trusted the brother, or sister, for that matter, who dismissed their Spanish roots so completely they'd taken on their stepfather's name and preferred the American versions of their own. The fact they had always treated Basilio like an unwanted distant cousin importuning them for favor, rather than a brother, wasn't in Carl's favor, either.

But family was family and Basilio never let his down. He wasn't about to start now.

His father had drilled family loyalty into Basilio his entire life, but more important, Basilio knew that his father would probably still be married to his first wife had it not been for the fact that Basilio's mother had gotten pregnant with him. Fidelity had never been Armand Perez's thing, but loyalty was. And he'd remained loyal to his wife until he had another child on the way at risk of becoming a bastard.

Basilio carried the weight of his family's dynamic on his shoulders.

Even if he was inclined to let his brother swing in the wind, Basilio would always protect the children of the family with the same commitment his father had shown Basilio. Armand Perez had given up the stability of his marriage, virtually lost all contact with his firstborn son and his precious daughter whom he still adored with a father's unconditional love, having to stand by while they took on another man's name. He'd lost the connections his wife's family offered to him and Perez Holdings, which had harbingered the beginning of the company's decline, and weathered scandal fueled by his wife's fury and desire for revenge.

All for the sake of an unborn son that Armand had never once laid any blame on, no matter what his first wife said in her more caustic moments, or Basilio's own brother and sister had on the few times they visited during his childhood.

While Armand still grieved the loss of his relationship and parental status with his two older children, he had never made Basilio feel like he was not enough, that his father had ever regretted, even for a minute, that he'd lost so much in order to claim Basilio.

It was a standard of adult commitment to the children of the family Basilio would live up to. Jamie and Grace were entirely innocent and deserving of every bit of Basilio's effort on their behalf.

"How are my nephew and niece?" he asked.

"The entire family is under stress."

"You have kept your children from the media, surely?"

"Jamie is in school. Other children talk."

"Well, keep him home until the furor dies down." Basilio knew his admonishment was too late in coming as the media furor was already on the wane, and Jamie must have already been subjected to it.

Basilio had had his own PR people apprise him of the latest mini-storm of media attention due to the reporter discovering Miranda's connection to a billionaire businessman.

"Don't be ridiculous," Carl said dismissively. "We're not calling him home and disrupting his schedule on account of that woman."

That was right. Jamie attended boarding school.

Something Basilio's father had not wanted for his own children, despite his wealth at the time of their childhood and his preoccupation with his paramours. "I would have thought it would be on his own account."

"Don't get sanctimonious with me," Carl barked. "He's my son and I'm doing my best to protect him."

"Are you?" Because from where Basilio sat, it seemed *he* was the one intent on protecting the child.

Carl hung up and Basilio put his own phone down with indifference.

His willingness to help was not reliant on his brother's warm regard.

Basilio was embarked on his current course for the sake of both his nine-year-old nephew and two-year-old niece. While Grace was unlikely to know what was happening, her home life wouldn't be pleasant if Miranda did the interview, and poor young Jamie would be subject to all sorts of scrutiny and comments at school. Again.

CHAPTER FOUR

STILL REELING FROM their whirlwind meeting and the amazing, unexpected, explosive, impulsive all-night sex marathon at one of Portland's most luxurious hotel suites, Randi waited impatiently for Basilio to pick her up so they could go look at properties for the second shelter site with his broker.

How had this billionaire, business shark, super-good-looking guy come into her life?

Really, what were the chances she would nearly mow down the guy of her dreams?

The fact he wouldn't make those dreams come true was something she was used to and not about to complain about. Randi practiced living in the moment these days, without too high of expectations for the future. She'd learned her lesson five years ago.

However, his insistence on helping her find a property? That was white-knight stuff she couldn't ignore.

Apparently, the Realtor she had been working with was not up to snuff as far as Baz was concerned and he'd ensured her that his recommended property broker would be happy to donate his commission on the sale, too. Impressed, she ran a mental list of the properties the broker had found already, properties the other Realtor had been convinced were not available at the price Kayla's for Kids could pay.

Her phone buzzed with a text. He was on his way up to her apartment. He could have just told her to come down, but not Basilio Perez. He knew how to treat a woman like she mattered, even if she was a very temporary fixture in his life.

Randi opened the door and looked down the hall toward the elevator just as Baz came through the door from the stairwell. Of course.

No elevators for only a couple of stories up for this man. He was just that guy. Doing everything better, stronger and faster than other mere mortals.

He'd changed into another tailored suit, his shirt now a deep burgundy instead of the traditional white he'd been wearing the day before. His lack of tie and the five o'clock shadow from his dark beard gave him a rakish air not quite fitting with

the head of a multinational real estate conglomerate.

But really, what did she know?

Maybe modern-day businessmen were just the
new era of pirates?

He slipped the phone he'd been texting on into
his suit pocket. "You have a strange expression on
your face, *cariña*. What is that about?"

"Um… I was picturing you as a pirate."

He startled, his dark eyes widening in surprise,
but then his head went back and he laughed. Long
and full, the sound was filled with genuine mirth.

"You don't think you're a pirate?" she asked with
her own smile.

He stopped laughing, his expression going more
serious than the thought warranted. "I'm sure there
are several business rivals, small property hold-
ers and employees that would say that is exactly
what I am."

An atavistic shiver went down her spine. "That's
a lot of people."

He shrugged. "My father had run Perez Holdings
into near bankruptcy by the time I was twenty.
There was no time for me to get an MBA. My education came in the cutthroat halls of big business."

"And you were determined to win?" This man would never accept anything less.

"For the sake of my family and the Perez name? Oh, yes, I was more than willing to become a pirate."

"You're kind of a ruthless guy, aren't you?" So different from her, and yet not.

Family was important to both of them. The welfare of children mattered to them both. During one of their hiatuses between sexual bouts, he'd told her he admired her career choice and believed children deserved the best the world could offer them.

"There is no *kind of* about it." He reached out and tucked a strand of her hair behind her ear. "There is no room for sentiment in business."

"Wow. I'm not sure I could dismiss people's feelings like that." And honestly, she had a hard time seeing him do it, too.

He reached for her jacket, lying over the back of her sofa, and held it up for her to put on. "You do what you have to when you are backed in a corner."

"I bet you didn't stay cornered for long." She flipped her hair from out of the jacket collar.

"You'd be surprised." Instead of going toward

the door, Baz stepped in closer to her. "Bringing Perez Holdings from bankruptcy to the multibillion-dollar international entity that it is today did not happen in a week, a month or even a couple of years."

"So does that ruthlessness translate to your interpersonal relationships?" she asked, breathless from his nearness and doing nothing to hide that fact.

That ship had sailed.

"I can be pitiless both on behalf of and *with* my family when it is necessary." There was no apology in his voice, no sense of regret at what he considered necessary action.

Suddenly realizing just how little she really knew about this man, Randi shivered.

Baz's brows knitted, his espresso eyes filling with concern. "Are you well?" he asked solicitously.

"Yes, of course." She'd just had another wake-up call, which she shouldn't have needed, but apparently did.

His hands landed warmly on her shoulders. "My father has been married many times, but the first time lasted the longest. She turned a blind eye to my father's infidelity and he was utterly loyal to her and my siblings."

"What happened?"

"I did." Baz looked surprised by his own admission. "My mother was my father's mistress, but she got pregnant and suddenly he had to weigh having a child of his grow up without his name and protection, or divorce."

"He chose divorce."

"*Sí.*" And from the look in Baz's dark gaze, he still carried a sense of responsibility for that fact.

"You know you were innocent in the choices your parents made, right?"

"Of course."

"Why don't I believe you?"

"I cannot say." He brushed his thumb up her neck, leaving shivers in the wake of the small caress. "Are you ready to go look at properties?"

"I am." Only didn't they have to step away from each other and, well, *leave the apartment* for that to happen?

"First things first, though." Oh, man, those dark eyes of his.

Who could resist them? Not her.

"Wha—?"

His lips cut off her inquiry, his mouth instantly heated and possessive against hers.

Despite knowing how all this was going to end, with him in Spain, probably with some gorgeous European supermodel, and Randi in Portland, doing what she'd always done, she gave herself to the kiss, allowing Baz to pull her into his arms without hesitation.

He held her close, his hands inside her coat, warm and sure against her back.

After several minutes of blissful loss of self, she made an instinctive protest when Baz stepped away.

He winked. Seriously. Winked. "If we don't leave now, we'll never get to all the properties on our agenda tonight."

The man was too delicious and good at kissing for her to be thinking logically right then. "And that's important."

"Isn't it?" he asked, his tone teasing and arousing at once.

She took a deep breath, let it out and forced her brain to function. "You know it is." She smiled. "And I appreciate your efforts on behalf of Kayla's for Kids a lot."

"While I believe in what your sister wanted to

do with these shelters, make no mistake, I've offered my help on your behalf."

Heat suffused her, but she wasn't losing her head again. "I can't believe your broker found such great possibilities."

"Sometimes, in real estate, it is who you know. Not all properties get listed on the MLS immediately. Some never do."

"That doesn't make any sense." It really didn't. "Wouldn't people want to have the biggest pool of potential buyers?"

"Sometimes the only buyer you need is the one who prefers exclusivity."

"But we're not looking for a multimillion-dollar property."

"No. Your budget is not exactly that of a pauper, either, however."

Funny, that wasn't the way her original Realtor had behaved. Her continuous message was that they needed to increase their budget, or lower their expectations.

"Besides," Baz went on, "you're buying on behalf of a nonprofit. If the seller is very wealthy or a corporate entity, they may be in a place where they desire the write-off of offering the property under market value. They save on capital gains as well as increasing their yearly tax shelter."

Okay, that did make sense. And was kind of smart, to boot.

Randi grabbed her backpack purse and slung it on. "Is that how the broker found properties in our price range that fulfilled most, if not all, the items on our wish list?"

They left the apartment, Randi turning off lights just before shutting and locking the door.

Baz answered her question on the way to the elevator. "I would assume so, yes."

"I'm beyond impressed."

"He's a very savvy guy. He wouldn't be working for me otherwise."

"That I believe."

He grinned, looking younger than his thirty years for a brief moment. "My reputation precedes me already."

She shook her head in wonder. "You're really confident, aren't you?"

"Some call me arrogant." And he didn't sound like that bothered him at all.

"That doesn't bother you at all?"

"Not particularly, no."

"You write your own rules to life." That was for sure.

"And you, whose rules do you live by?"

Randi wasn't sure she had an answer to that. She'd spent so much of her adult life, and early childhood, reacting.

"I think I live by the rule of survival."

"So then, we have that in common. The survival of the Perez name, my family's survival, my company's survival, these are paramount to me."

They were on their way to the first property when she asked about the family he kept mentioning as being so important.

Baz cast her a sidelong glance as he pulled the luxury car to a smooth stop at a red light. "My father maintains a nominal position in the company while he negotiates his fifth marriage."

"That's a lot of wives. He must have tons of kids." And pay a lot of alimony.

No wonder the man's company had been doing so poorly.

"Actually, there are only three of us." Baz pulled into traffic again, his olive-toned hands curled loosely around the leather steering wheel.

"Are you close to the others?" Randi asked,

thinking how much she wished she'd grown up with Kayla as part of her life.

"Not really. My older brother and sister were content to keep to themselves once our father divorced their mother." There was something subtle in Baz's tone that implied pain at that truth, despite his nonchalant attitude.

"I'm sorry to hear that." She laid her hand on his thigh in what she hoped was comfort. "Finding Kayla is one of the best things that has happened in my life."

"That is a sweet sentiment."

But he didn't do sentiment and maybe she understood his stand on that a little better. A dad who went through wives like disposable commodities, siblings who ignored his existence and a young adulthood spent learning life's lessons in the merciless school of big business, Baz had little opportunity to appreciate the softer emotions.

"What about your mom?"

"She married my father for his money and negotiated their prenup with more acuity than any woman or man I've faced across a conference table, with lawyers lining both sides."

"She knew her marriage had a sell-by date."

"She was smart enough to realize that even

though she was only the second wife, she would not be the last."

"What about her relationship with you?"

"I lived with my father after the divorce."

"What? Why?"

"His first wife had taken his children to another country. He insisted on that provision in the pre-nup. In exchange for a very generous divorce settlement, he got primary custody."

"That must have been heartbreaking for both of you."

"Not so much. She got visitation, and my father, for all his womanizing ways, was a decent parent."

"My mother kept my sister from me. I didn't even know about her until this last year. I'm not sure I'll ever forgive her for that." Not to mention other things her mother had done that kept her firmly out of the running for decent human being, much less Mother of the Year.

"My father did not keep me from my siblings, or from my mother."

But someone had, at least from his siblings. Because she could read between the lines and the message there was that Baz did not feel like he was a part of their family, despite how *he* saw them.

"Your loyalty to your family is surprisingly strong."

"My father may have failed spectacularly at marriage, but his familial loyalty to his own parents, siblings, wives, ex-wives and children was and is absolute. He required no less from me."

Add that to the guilt Baz so obviously carried in regard to his father's first marriage's breakup, that made for some compelling motivation for his sense of loyalty toward people that might not deserve it.

"But not your siblings?" She also had to assume that by familial loyalty, Baz did not mean sexual fidelity. Or there wouldn't have been four ex-wives to this point.

"After taking them back to her own country after the divorce, their mother remarried quickly. They didn't just take on their stepfather's last name. They were raised with a different set of values."

"You're more understanding than I would have thought considering your pirate nature." She used the small tease to lighten the suddenly heavy atmosphere in the car.

"Yes, well, I can be surprising."

"You've shocked my socks off since meeting, that's for sure."

He cast her a heated glance. "It's not merely your socks I'm keen to see you out of."

Randi blushed to the roots of her hair. Darn him. "You didn't get enough of that last night?" Or that morning? They'd been intimate again after breakfast, necessitating a second shower before checking out of the hotel suite.

"I believe I have already told you that one night would not be enough."

"Lucky me."

"I am glad you think so, though I consider myself the one favored by fortune."

She patted his thigh, hard muscles bunching under her fingers, distracting her and forcing her to think about what she was going to say. Oh, that was right. "I wouldn't have taken you for a sweet-talker."

"I am not. I mean what I say." His hand settled over hers, pressing them both more firmly against his leg.

She sucked in air at how quickly she got turned on by that simple move. "And I'm glad to hear that."

They toured two properties, the banter between

them never abating, and were now in the third facility.

"It looks like a school," she said uncertainly. On paper this property had all the room the shelter required, but she'd never considered it might be an institutional building.

"It was a boarding school. The remodel necessary for your purposes would be minimal. The entire second floor is already living quarters. The classrooms, offices and public spaces dovetail into your vision for this new Kayla's for Kids."

She loved that he'd paid such close attention to the things she'd told him.

When they got inside, she saw exactly what he meant. The building was in surprisingly good repair and offered everything she could want for the housing of hard-to-place foster care children and homeless teens, and offering after-school activities to even more at-risk youth.

She stared around the dining hall, shocked it was still furnished with tables and chairs. "Is there a note the furnishings are for sale, as well?"

"They are."

"The seller would probably want more than our budget."

Baz referred to something on his phone. "She's

a seventy-year-old very wealthy philanthropist. My guess is when she finds out what you want to do with the property, she'll either offer the furnishings for nothing or well under market value."

Randi got the best kind of chills. "You think so?"

"I do. She was instrumental in funding the school as well as providing the facility."

"She sounds like an amazing lady."

"Perhaps we can arrange a personal meeting if you buy this property. It never hurts to have another benefactor for a nonprofit."

Randi stepped closer to Baz, taking his lapels in her fists. "You're always thinking, aren't you?"

"*Si* is a word I like. *No*, not so much." His sexy grin sent thrills through her.

She huffed out a laugh. "I totally believe it."

An hour later, after a quick text exchange with Kayla that included a ton of pictures, Randi and Baz had worked out an offer for the property with his broker.

"I'm certain this will be accepted, particularly once we apprise the seller of what you are buying the property for." The broker shook first Baz's hand and then Randi's, showing that despite her being the buyer, he knew who buttered the broker's bread.

"Shall we go out to celebrate a successful evening's work?" Baz asked when they reached his silver metallic sports model Mercedes.

"I don't want to jinx it by celebrating too early."

"Surely you are too well educated and intelligent for such superstitions." The locks snicked and Baz opened the passenger-side door for her.

She slid into her seat, but looked up at him as he leaned against the open door. "No one is too educated or smart to learn life's lessons."

"And you have learned that dreams do not always come true?"

"I told you I have."

"But not why."

Last night she couldn't imagine sharing one of the worst times in her life with this man, a practical stranger. After he'd helped her, shared insights into his own life and, well…made love to her so many times, he didn't feel like a stranger anymore.

She brushed her hand over the leather dash of the Mercedes as Baz climbed into the driver's seat. "I wouldn't have thought you could rent a car like this by the week."

"Money makes many things possible."

The fact that he didn't pressure her further into sharing confidences took away the last of Randi's reservations about doing so.

"Five years ago I was driving back to my dorm at the university after visiting my dad." She was glad they were in the car for privacy, but she wished he was driving. Meeting his eyes right now was hard, but she did it. "The street I was on only had a thirty-mile-an-hour speed limit and I was going under. I was always cautious because as well as businesses, there were houses and apartments along that stretch."

Baz made no move to put his seat belt on or start the car, but stayed facing her, his focus entirely on Randi. "And?"

"And a little boy ran out from between two parked cars. He'd been with his mother at a park two blocks away. She had no idea he was gone until she heard the sirens."

"What?" Baz looked shocked, his olive complexion going pale.

An understandable reaction to where the conversation was obviously going, she thought.

"I couldn't stop fast enough." She paused, taking several shallow breaths. This never got easier to talk about. Randi wasn't even sure she would have told Kayla until the whole fiasco a few weeks ago when a reporter discovered that Randi Smith used to be Randi Weber from Southern California. "There were cars in the oncoming lane and parked cars beside me. I had nowhere to go. Though I tried. I still clipped that tiny body with my car. It was the most horrific moment of my life."

Even worse than the terror and emotional agony she'd felt when her mother had tried to drown her when Randi was six.

"I would imagine." There was a strange quality to Baz's voice.

"Believe me when I say I'd had other terrifying moments, but nothing that compared."

"Was the child okay?"

"Eventually. He was in a coma for weeks and he had to learn how to speak and walk again once he woke up. It was my worst nightmare." It would have been anyone's.

"You say there was nothing you could have done?" The still quality to Baz's voice gave Randi pause.

And made her feel defensive, which surprised her. She shouldn't be, though. His reacting with understanding would have been the true shock, wouldn't it? No one else had. Not until Kayla and Andreas learned about what had happened.

"No, there was nothing."

"So?"

"Do you think knowing I had no options makes me feel better? That I haven't gone over those two seconds in my mind a million times, looking for a different outcome? There wasn't one, but it didn't matter. Not when his parents turned their PR machine on to the task of discrediting me. I guess they didn't want anyone to know it was the mom's fault."

"She did not hit him with her car."

Randi felt those words like a blow and had to look away from him. "No, she didn't, but no child of four should have been on that street unaccompanied." She looked back, her face tight with anger she would no longer hide, not out of misplaced compassion for the Madisons, people who had shown they had absolutely none for her. "The doctors said that if I'd been going the speed limit, he would be dead. His tiny body was no competition for even my eco-friendly subcompact."

"He would not have been, no." There was definitely a dark overtone in both Baz's words and manner.

"The papers, news reports, people all over social media, they all took your attitude."

"My attitude?" he asked.

"They believed it was all my fault. I must have been driving recklessly or not paying attention. The Madisons made sure that was the message being fed to every outlet. Mrs. Madison played the victim very well."

"She was a victim, surely. Her child was in the hospital."

She was going to be sick. She should have been prepared for this, but she wasn't. "And that is why despite the police ruling it an unavoidable accident, despite screen shots and traffic cams that proved she was negligent, I said nothing. I knew she must be going through hell and I wasn't taking her through more. Not even with the truth."

"If she was negligent, she would have been charged."

Unbelievable. Okay, they'd only slept together one night, but didn't she deserve even a tiny bit more consideration than a complete stranger? "By that same argument, then I must have been innocent, right? After all, if I was the monster the Madisons painted me, wouldn't they have taken me to civil court, even if the DA declined to prosecute?"

"That is a point, yes."

Could he have been any more skeptical in his tone?

Randi was definitely regretting telling this piece of painful history to the man with the stony expression. "You still think it was my fault."

"I did not say that." But his attitude and the expression in his espresso eyes did.

"Would you please take me back to my apartment?"

"Does it matter so much what I think?"

"I've had my fill of being judged a monster when there was more than enough blame to go around." She knew better than to open herself for more of the same.

She'd been a fool to think it was safe sharing one of her most painful secrets with a temporary sexual partner, regardless of his help in finding a home for the Kayla's for Kids shelter.

"Are you going to do something about it?" he asked.

"As a matter of fact, I am. I have plans to set the record straight with the media."

"People have already made up their minds, according to you. What difference will a press release make?"

"An interview, on national television, not a press release." Which was overwhelming and scary to think about, not that she would offer that proof of more vulnerability to him. "I'll get to tell my side, the truth."

That was what was important. She had to remember that.

"Why would you put the family through that?"

Seriously? The family angle again? She supposed to a man so steeped in obligation toward family it made sense, but what about her? What about what *her* family had been through when she'd been vilified for behavior she'd never engaged in: reckless driving, inattention, not caring?

"You don't think it's fair?" she demanded skeptically. "After the media crucified me because of the story the Madisons fed them, I lost my almost fiancé, my scholarship and my position at the university. To achieve any measure of peace and anonymity in my life, I had to give up my last name and move away from my father and grandparents. Now the Madisons are trying to do it all over again. I'm not giving up another thing for their sensibilities."

"What do you mean they're trying to do it again? What are they doing?" he asked like the answer really mattered.

She wasn't buying that bridge. Not again. But she didn't mind telling him. It wasn't a state secret. "Their best to keep the truth under wraps, to make me their scapegoat again."

"Trying to find peace after such a tragedy is hardly making you the scapegoat," he scoffed.

Was this really the man she'd shared her body with the night before? The same man who had worked so hard to find the best property for her without anything in it for him? "What would you call threatening to destroy my *new* life?"

"The attempt to protect his family by a desperate man."

"Oh, my gosh, you don't even know these people, but you're their champion?"

He frowned, looking almost guilty. "It is clearly an untenable situation for everyone."

"I guess I should be grateful you include me in that *everyone*."

"It was a terrible time in your life. That accident cost you a great deal. I would have to be blind not to see that."

"You think?"

His lips twisted with frustration. "Yes, I do. However, I do not think bringing it all back up in front of the national media, no less, is going to make your life better. It will certainly hurt a family that has already been through hell, especially their children. The young can be so cruel."

She had firsthand experience with just how cruel *adults* could be. "And the hell I've been through?"

"Won't disappear by opening yourself up to further comment and potential vilification."

"You don't think it matters if the truth comes out?"

"I don't think it will help you, or them." He reached across the console, cupping her cheek. "Don't stir it all up again."

She jerked her face away from touch that should not be comforting. "I'm not the one doing that."

"Then who?"

"First it was a small article written for one of the online news media, nothing that really got a lot of attention, but then somehow Mr. Madison became aware of it, and before I knew what was happening, I was being trolled on the only social page I keep. Other articles started popping up, all with a heavy slant to what *my* supposed carelessness had cost the Madison family. It was five years ago all over again, only this time Mr. Madison came to me personally. He threatened me, threatened to get me fired."

"He didn't realize you work for your sister?" Baz sounded disgusted by such incompetence.

It would have been funny in another situation.

"No. We've never shared the same last name. Only the people closest to us even know we're sisters."

"And you threatened him back," Baz guessed, proving he had no inkling of who Randi really was.

"No. Not at all. I told him to leave, but he wouldn't. He had some goon with him, a big man who wouldn't let me leave, either."

"This goon, did he restrain you?" Now Baz sounded furious.

She couldn't imagine why.

"He and Mr. Madison. I screamed. Carl Madison slapped me. I was terrified. He said he was going to make people believe I had abused the children I worked with. He said what was left of my life wasn't going to be worth living when he was done with me."

"That is not..." His voice trailed off, the expression on Baz's face murderous. "Did you file charges for assault?"

"Not at first. I was so used to feeling guilty, to believing the Madison family needed protecting after what had happened to Jamie, that's the name of the boy, I just broke down. The goon threw me on the floor, and after a few more vicious threats that made me wonder if my life was seriously in danger, they left."

"And then?"

"And then I went home."

"But somehow you got from there to here."

"That was Kayla. I was still shaken up the next day when we had a meeting about Kayla's for Kids. She pried the whole story out of me, and for the first and only time, someone learned about the horrible day without judging me a monster."

"I do not think you are a monster."

She wasn't touching that denial. Randi knew what she'd seen in his eyes. "She and Andreas convinced me to press charges. Not that it did much good. Mr. Madison has a whole bevy of expensive lawyers on his side. He got a plea deal that allowed for a misdemeanor, settled with a fine. Andreas was adamant I take out a restraining order after that."

"So you did."

"Yes. Andreas may be a shark like you, but he cares about people's feelings and he was livid about the way I'd been treated. He's the one who set up the interview on the morning talk show."

"Your hero." There was no mistaking the sardonic tone to Baz's voice.

"Yes, finally I had one."

"Not your own father?"

"Dad is a high school English teacher. He had to change schools after what happened. His principal was one of the people who thought I was a monster and he let Dad know it. No, my dad never doubted me. Neither did my grandparents, but none of them could help me. Not in the face of the Madison wealth and influence."

She swallowed against the tightening in her throat and blinked back tears. "That's not to say they didn't help me at all. Dad made sure I got into another school. They all pitched in to help support me while I made the move to Sacramento. It was my dad's idea to change my last name. I took his mom's maiden name, but couldn't get a job until all the paperwork cleared the courts and I got my new identification."

"And then there was your lost scholarship."

"Yes. My grandparents joined with Dad to keep me in school. I worked, too, but I never would have gotten my degree in social work without them."

"Do you think you chose to help children because you felt guilty about what happened to Jamie?" he asked, for once not sounding judgmental, just curious.

"No. I know exactly why I got into the field I did and it had little to nothing to do with what happened five years ago."

"What, then?"

"You've gotten all the confidences you're going to get out of me."

"Do not be like that. I told you, I do not judge you."

No, he'd said he didn't think she was a monster and Randi hadn't believed him. "Believe it or not, your opinion makes very little difference to me."

"I do not believe, *cariña*."

"Don't call me that."

"Why not? You think because you shared this burden we are now going to go our separate ways like we never met?"

Yep, that was the plan. "You think the sex was good enough to justify having more with a woman you believe responsible for a small boy ending up in the hospital. I don't have to agree with that sentiment."

"What I think is that you are unnecessarily defensive about something that has caused you enough pain. Do not allow the sharing of it to cut off the pleasure we find in one another's company."

That was not what she was doing, was it? No. "You defended them. I'm the woman you slept with, but when I told you, your whole concern was for the Madisons."

"I apologize that is how it seemed. It is not the case. You matter to me, Miranda. Your feelings matter to me and our time together is not over."

"You don't make any sense." But hearing she mattered soothed the rough edges of the wounds he'd inflicted with his attitude.

"I make perfect sense. I told you this was no one-night stand."

"Even after what you just heard?"

"Especially after that. Right now you could use another friend and we are good together. A tragedy in your past does not change that."

Did he really believe that? "You defended people who did everything they could to destroy my life. How is that being my friend?"

"Do not hold my ability to see both sides of this situation against me. Especially when it was your own compassion toward the Madisons that allowed you to remain silent so long."

Okay, maybe he had a point. "You're sure you see *both* sides?"

"Do not doubt it."

She pulled her seat belt across her body and snapped it in the lock. "I'll work on the not doubting thing, but right now could you please take me back to my apartment?"

"If that is what you truly desire."

"It is."

CHAPTER FIVE

BAZ IGNORED MIRANDA'S obvious hints that he needn't park the car, but could just drop her off in front of the apartment complex.

Instead, he found a spot under a light in the visitor section of the parking lot and turned off the engine.

She unclipped her seat belt, her focus on the dark night out the window. "I'm not really in the mood for more company."

"I will walk you up." He'd work on her desire to get rid of him once he was in her apartment. He'd messed up spectacularly when he'd allowed his natural inclination to defend his family rise to the surface.

It wasn't like him to make a mistake like that, but when he was around Miranda, Basilio found himself showing more of the man who lived inside the corporate shark's body than with anyone else. Even the family with which he was currently damn angry.

With the exception of his nephew and niece. They continued to be the innocent victims in a terrible situation that should never have had the cost to Miranda's life it had, but should definitely not be allowed to destroy theirs, either.

"That's not necessary."

"I think it is."

She rolled her eyes, but didn't argue further. However, for the first time that evening, she did not wait for him to come around and open her car door, but got out of the Mercedes immediately, closing her door with more force than necessary.

She was angry. And he did not blame her. As far as she knew, he *had* defended a complete stranger over the woman who had shared his bed with so much passion the night before.

If her story was true—and despite the fact he'd only known her a short while and his family was, well…his family, he believed her—then she had good reason to despise his brother *and* his sister-in-law. Miranda had taken the high road five years before, protecting people who had been indisputably vile to her when she had shown them nothing but compassion.

Regardless, however, Basilio had not been lying when he told her that doing the interview would not serve her. The media furor was dying down and stirring it up again would do her no favors, no matter what the truth was.

Basilio could easily verify Miranda's accusations against his brother. Police records were not something that could be dismissed with a plausible story by Carlos. Which meant Basilio's older brother had assaulted Miranda and made heinous threats. He had not simply begged her to let things die down and give their family peace, as both Gracia and Carlos claimed.

Basilio was beyond angry at the prospect he'd been lied to by his family, but he was even more furious about what his brother had done to Miranda. He would be calling Carlos later and letting him know just how unacceptable his behavior had been, but right now it was time to mend fences with Miranda.

Because he could not alter his course in trying to convince Miranda to cancel the interview, though. Not for her sake, and not for the sake of Basilio's family. While the adults might not deserve his protection, his innocent niece and nephew did. And while they were called Madisons, the Perez name was at stake, as well.

"You're awfully quiet now." She sounded suspicious.

He could not blame her. He did, in fact, have plans and she was an intelligent woman.

"Am I?" he asked as they exited the elevator on her floor. He preferred the stairs, but she'd made it clear she intended to take the conveyance.

"You had plenty to say earlier."

"Too much if I've offended you so much you no longer want my company." He'd been so shocked by Miranda's claim the accident happened because of Tiffany's apparent neglect to Jamie's welfare, he'd gone into family protection mode immediately.

Shown too much of himself to the woman whom he found it too easy to do that with.

At first, he hadn't even wanted to believe Tiffany had been at fault, but he'd come around fast. Miranda simply was not a dishonest woman, which made her vulnerable to people like Basilio's brother, who did not care if they had to use lies to protect an unpleasant secret.

It made sense of the fact that Basilio never saw Tiffany with the children without the nanny. He'd thought it rather affected that the nanny even accompanied her on visits to her mother's home.

Now he wondered if that was because no one trusted her to watch her own children with proper diligence.

And what did that say about the unleashing of the Madison PR machine on the hapless nineteen-year-old Miranda?

Nothing good, that was for damn sure.

Miranda stopped outside her door and turned to face Basilio, but she made no effort to meet his gaze. "I'll say good-night now. Maybe you can call me tomorrow." She didn't sound like she thought there was even a remote chance of that happening.

And she was right, but not for the reasons this beautiful, vulnerable and entirely too compassionate woman thought. "I'll see you inside." He had every hope of being there in the morning.

"I don't think that's a good idea."

"Please, *mi hermosa*. Do not do this." He never pleaded, but right now it was his job to equalize things between them.

And if that required him swallowing a tiny bite of his Spanish pride, so be it.

Finally, her head tilted up, her expressive gray eyes clouded with emotion. "Why?"

"You can ask that after last night?" He paused, letting his words sink in. "And this morning?"

"That's sex. You can get it elsewhere. So can I."

Chance would be a fine thing. As far as Basilio's investigators could tell, the woman had been celibate since her last disastrous relationship five years previous.

"Not that kind of sex. Not the mind-blowing, expectation-smashing joining of two bodies." He moved in on her, pressing her back against her door, watching for denial that never came. "What we experience together is something special."

"For you?" she demanded with clear disbelief.

"*Sí*. Do not doubt it."

Miranda shook her head, her golden-brown hair rubbing against the door. He kissed her before she could say something they would both regret, like that he should leave. Which he would do if she requested.

After her recount of what had happened with Carlos, Basilio refused to do anything that might spark similar fear in her.

But Miranda did not fight the kiss, or even refuse to respond. Her mouth went soft against his with a sound that was very much like surrender. Relief all out of proportion for the situation shot through him.

Basilio reached down to where she held the keys

in her hand and gently took them. Without breaking the kiss, he found the proper key for the locks through trial and error, and finally the door swung open behind her.

Miranda stumbled backward and he followed, closing the door behind them. The way to her room was strewn with discarded clothes as they kissed with a passion so much bigger than what he felt with other women. He hadn't been blowing smoke up her skirt when he said this kind of sex was special for him; it was entirely outside his undeniably sufficient experience.

He'd had enough women in his bed to know that finding one so compatible, so combustible, was extraordinary. So rare, he'd never actually coupled with a woman he was so instantly into, or one whose kiss could have him so close to coming without even a touch to his sex.

By the time they reached the bedroom, Miranda was down to another sexy set of lingerie and he was completely nude.

"As tantalizing as these are, there is no place for any covering between us when we reach that bed." He pointed to the full-size bed stacked high with colorful pillows and covered in a spread that looked like it might have come from India.

She measured him with her gray gaze. "Then maybe you should take them off."

He didn't need a second invitation, reaching out to do exactly as she suggested. In a matter of seconds the final bits of clothing were lying on the floor, and nothing hindered his gaze from consuming her elegant curves, the way her nipples were already taut and flushed with need, the glistening patch of curls at the apex of her thighs.

"You are truly beautiful."

"English tonight?"

"Probably not for long." She made him lose his ability to communicate in anything but the most primitive.

A shadow seemed to lift from her, as if his admission had given her some kind of reassurance. He was glad he had allowed truth to speak in that case.

Her bore her back to the bed, her soft thighs a cradle for his hard muscles, her hands coming up to grip the back of his head.

Their kiss went incendiary and the hours that followed were even better than the night before. What sleep they got, they spent wrapped in each other. There was really no choice, not in the double bed that wasn't really meant for two people.

Especially when one of them was six foot four and broad-shouldered, and showed a heretofore unknown tendency to cuddle.

In the middle of the night, he woke to her touching him and was so damn turned on by her initiating their lovemaking that he didn't even think of the condom until after he'd climaxed in her tight, wet heat.

He didn't actually think of it until she started swearing, which so far he'd never heard her do, and then pounding on his shoulder. "Move. Get off me. We forgot the condom! I can't believe this. It's not happening. *We forgot the condom.*"

Despite the urgency in her tone, he was careful as he withdrew from her body. Basilio rolled to his side, but didn't jump from the bed and held her wrist when it was clear that was what she wanted to do. "Don't have a fit."

She yanked her arm away and sat up, turning on the light. "How can you say that? We just had *unprotected sex.* I've never even asked to see test results from you. I can't believe I didn't. Kayla keeps reminding me I need to be safe, but I never thought it would come up. I wasn't even dating anyone!"

"Calm down, *bella.* You are fine. *We* are fine.

I can show you the results of my latest physical."
He counted it a win that she'd stayed in the bed.

"How long ago was that? More important, how many women? Did you have sex with *them* without protection?" The questions came fast and furious, her lovely gray eyes wild.

"No. Never before. You have nothing to concern yourself with."

But she was freaking out, her body strung like a bow, tension emanating off her in stress-filled waves. Her pupils were blown with shock, not pleasure. Unfortunately.

"Of course I'm going to concern myself. I can't believe I never asked to see anything before. What's the matter with me?" she practically shrieked. "I totally fail at this modern woman reveling in her independence thing."

He would have laughed if she hadn't said the last with such a sense of despondency. "You are getting hysterical for no reason."

"I'm not hysterical!" She shot him the glare of death. "How can you say that? I don't get hysterical."

Okay. Sure. "So, I can see."

"Don't patronize me." She smacked the bed

for emphasis, the sheet covering her breasts slipping down.

He reached out and readjusted the bedding, tugging it up and tucking it around her. "You must stop this spiraling. Trust me, you have nothing to fear from me."

"What about pregnancy? What about that?"

Alarm coursed through him. "You're not on birth control?" What woman today did not protect herself from unplanned pregnancies?

Maybe a celibate one. He'd read the report; he should have paid attention to what that meant.

"No! I told you, I suck at this!"

"The only kind of sucking you do is very pleasurable and wholly positive."

"This is not a joke!" She was spiraling again.

"Of course not." He reached out, going to touch her again, relieved when she didn't pull away this time. He put his hand against her neck and let it slide down to cup her shoulder. "There is the morning-after pill."

"Yes. Right. Yes. Where do I get that?" She looked around wildly, like she expected to find one lying on the nightstand or dresser.

He bit back another smile. "At the pharmacy, I would imagine."

"Oh, right. Of course." She reached over and grabbed her phone off the bedside table. Soon she was lost to whatever she was reading on the screen. "It says here for the one I don't need a prescription for, I've got three days. That's good, right?"

"Sí, esta bien."

"But it also says that even the one that is good for up to five days doesn't work if I'm already ovulating. What if I am?"

"Do not assume the worst." He tried to see what she was reading on her phone, but the text was too tiny. "People try for years to get pregnant and don't manage it. There's no reason to think one transgression is going to result in you carrying my child."

The thought of it, though? Was more alluring than alarming.

Ridiculous.

Basilio squashed that train of thought fast. While he knew a great deal more about Miranda than she realized, courtesy of the report he'd had compiled on her, they'd only met the day before. Great sex did not equate to a relationship solid enough to build a family on.

If he'd learned nothing else from his father's serial infidelity, Basilio knew that to be true.

"It says here... Oh, my goodness... I'm right in the middle of when I should be ovulating." She looked at him with stricken eyes. "I'm not ready to be a mom. I don't know if I ever will be."

A woman who dedicated her life to children didn't want any of her own? How was that possible? "Stop borrowing trouble. Please. We will go to the pharmacy as soon as it opens in the morning if that will make you feel better."

"But what good will it do? I've probably already ovulated."

"We'll call the doctor. Maybe he will have a solution."

"My doctor is a woman."

"She, then."

"Okay, okay, we'll have to wait for tomorrow." But she didn't sound like she was going to survive without losing it during the interim.

"Miranda, *mi hermosa*." He waited for her to acknowledge him.

When she didn't, seeming to be lost in a world of potential unplanned pregnancies, he got up from the bed. She still didn't act like she even realized he was still in the room, so he went into her bathroom, where there was thankfully a surprisingly large tub. The apartment complex was old and the porcelain tub looked original to the building, deeper and slightly wider than those he'd seen in more modern dwellings of the same caliber.

Basilio ran a bath, pouring some salts into the water from a stash he'd found under the sink. When he went back into the bedroom, Miranda was still sitting on the bed, her slightly out of focus expression filled with dismay.

"I ran you a bath."

"You think that will help?"

"I do."

"How? You think the hot water will somehow miraculously render your swimmers inert? Somehow, I don't see it."

"You need to relax," he clarified. "It will help with that."

She stared at him like she was trying to read something in his gaze. Finally, she nodded.

Miranda allowed him to lead her into the now-steamy bathroom, her hand limp in his. This lost and dispirited Miranda wasn't one he recognized, and frankly, it bothered him.

Sinking into the hot water, she sighed as if releasing tension, but her mouth remained flat, her eyes still unfocused.

Basilio bathed his beautiful lover, being careful not to let his touches grow sexual, no matter how the sight of her naked body incited his own flesh. Finally, after several minutes of him cupping the hot water and letting it pour down her skin, Miranda collapsed against the angled back of the tub, letting her body slide down so most of it was submerged.

Since there were no bubbles, the submersion did his libido no favors.

Still, he managed to control himself as he spoke to her about everything but sex, babies and her past.

At first, her responses were desultory or disjointed by turns, but eventually she began to share in the conversation, expressing the opinion that autumn wasn't really autumn without the leaves changing color. It was a throwaway conversation, but her willingness to engage made Basilio nearly weak with relief.

She'd really been thrown by them having unprotected sex and coming to the realization they'd shared nothing of their health status with each other.

Understandable, really. She knew almost nothing about him. He, on the other hand, had walked into this with plenty of information on Miranda Smith, née Weber. The report on her had included her recent sexual activity, or lack thereof, and her health status. The first time they had sex, he'd known he didn't need to see test results.

She'd let her desire override good sense.

He'd done exactly the same thing when he woke up beside her, his mind filled with the memory dreams he'd been having.

He wasn't sure why he wasn't as disturbed by the prospect of her being pregnant as she was, but Miranda was definitely not a woman who took this kind of situation in stride.

Her lack of practical knowledge about the morning-after pill only showed what he'd suspected. Miranda Smith simply did not take risks like the one they'd taken. A very primitive part of him liked knowing she was out of control when they had sex as he'd proved himself to be.

It made no sense in their situation. Their interlude couldn't last. There was too much standing between them for him to even consider a long-distance relationship with this woman.

Yet he found more satisfaction in bathing her

than he did in intercourse with many of his past lovers. Her silky skin. Her soft, modest curves. It was all perfect.

Miranda suddenly rose up from the hot water, leaving him scrambling to his feet.

"I'll take the morning-after pill, but if I've already ovulated, it's not going to work." Water glistened on her silky skin.

He had to focus on what she'd said rather than the body he found so perfect. Okay, they were back to unplanned baby prospect for conversation. "Think positive."

"I've learned to be a realist." She stepped out of the draining water and onto the bath mat.

"But you are naturally optimistic. I hear it in the way you talk about the children you're trying to help." He reached out to dry her off with the towel he'd grabbed from the rack.

She took the brightly colored terry cloth from him, stepping as far away as she could in the limited space. "I have hope for them."

"But not yourself?"

"I'm not unhappy." She finished drying off and wrapped the towel around her torso, hiding her nudity from him.

The action felt significant.

"No." He reached for her hand, holding it as he led the way back into the bedroom, inexplicably grateful when she let him. "But you think the worst will happen."

"Is a baby the worst thing? I guess you'd think so."

"That is not what I said." Damn. She was adept at reading meaning into the least word.

"But it's what you meant."

"No."

"So you're saying that if I'm pregnant, you'll be part of the baby's life."

He didn't suggest other more definitive answers to an unwanted pregnancy. He could read between the lines, too, and hopefully with more accuracy. Despite what it would surely mean for her life, Miranda wouldn't consider the baby unwanted.

"I would, yes." His own child would trump his brother's sensibilities. It would be a way to keep Miranda in Basilio's life.

He did his best to quash the foolish thought, but it would not go away.

She stopped beside the bed and faced him. "You're serious?"

"We may not know each other well, but you are already aware of how loyal I am to my family."

Tension drained out of her, her lovely face relaxing, her body losing its too-tense posture. "Okay, good. Not that I think I'm pregnant."

She could have fooled him.

"I mean, what are the chances one time would do it?" she asked like he hadn't brought up that very point before. "People try for years for children."

He'd mentioned that, too, but he wasn't going to remind her. She was finally coming down off the ledge.

"Are you ready to go back to bed?" They had at least a couple of hours before they needed to get up.

She resisted his tug that would have resulted in her sitting on the edge of the bed. "Um, do you have access to your health status on your phone?"

"Of course." What sexually active person in today's world didn't?

"Great. Um…can I see it?"

He nearly smacked his own forehead in a moment of realization. Of course she wanted that. He should have thought of it as soon as she mentioned not seeing them earlier. "*No problemo.* Let me pull it up."

"Um… I've got mine, too."

"And you will show me and then you will relax, hmm?"

"Maybe?" She got her phone from the charger beside the bed.

It only took a minute for them to look at one another's phones.

"So you haven't, um, had other unprotected sex…you know, since your last physical?"

"No." He would have told her that he'd never had unprotected sex before, because it was true, but that might make her think there was something more between them.

Something beyond sex unlike anything he'd ever known. Something possibly permanent when they could be anything but.

"You don't regularly engage in high-risk behavior?" She sounded like she was repeating something she'd read.

He answered her regardless. "No, I do not."

"Okay, good. That's good." She gave him a severely uncomfortable look. "You can ask me, too."

"You would not have freaked out so badly if this was something you were used to."

Her expression cleared, like she was relieved he wouldn't be asking her personal questions about her sex life. "That's true. I'm glad you realize that."

"You already told me you aren't easy."

"I could have been lying."

"I do not think lying is something you do often, or well." Which was why Basilio had believed her about the day five years ago and Tiffany's part in it, as well as Miranda's claims about his brother's abhorrent behavior.

"You're right." She bit her bottom lip, her manner vulnerable. "I hate dishonesty."

A frisson of unexpected concern went through him. She was not going to take well to learning that there had been an ulterior motive behind their meeting. *If* she ever learned it. He couldn't be naive to the possibility, though. She was too intelligent for him to dismiss the chance.

Danger of exposure or not, he had a job to do.

For her sake now as much as for Basilio's family.

He needed to convince Miranda to cancel that interview. Basilio could not allow himself to be sidetracked by her addictive reaction in bed, or even the possibility of pregnancy.

If she thought Carlos had ruined her life already, it would be nothing compared to opening herself up to the haters and the gossip hounds that would come out of the woodwork once she did an interview on national television.

Ask any celebrity, politician or person of interest who lived under the scrutiny of the paparazzi. People interested in scandal could be much more ruthless than Basilio in pursuing their own agendas. They were not interested in truth, only stories that increased their ratings, circulation or viral presence online.

Not that Carlos and his PR people wouldn't have to make concessions, too. Now that Basilio knew the truth of what happened five years before, he wasn't going to allow them to smear Miranda's name any longer. He, more than anyone, understood the power of reputation, and Miranda had worked as hard as he in her own way to rebuild hers.

But he'd warned her that ruthlessness was part of his makeup. What he hadn't said was that he could be downright brutal when pursuing a goal, as many had learned to their detriment in the years since he'd taken over his father's company.

Including his father's ex-wives, who were used to asking for money beyond what they were legally entitled to, whenever they wanted. He'd cut off any payments other than what was outlined in each divorce decree. It had infuriated his various stepmothers, but they'd settled down when he'd told them he had already put the entire company in his own name, making his father a pauper on paper, and then threatened to take them back to court to adjust alimony payments.

Even his own mother had learned to live within the bounds of the generous monthly allowance she received.

And Basilio had never once regretted the hard choices he had to make. Until now. While he would not allow it to change the outcome, he hated the thought of Miranda's passionate acceptance turning to distrust.

So he would just have to make sure that did not happen.

CHAPTER SIX

ANTICIPATION RIDING HER like an experienced jockey, refusing to be dislodged no matter how much she tried, Randi shut down her computer.

She shouldn't be looking forward to seeing Baz so much. It was dangerous.

They had plans when she got off work. Just like they had every evening for the past week.

They'd had dinner a second time with Andreas and Kayla to celebrate the seller accepting Kayla's for Kids' offer for the new property. Baz had been right and the owner had donated the furnishings that had not been moved to their new school facility. They'd been to the Pompeii exhibit at the Oregon Museum of Science and Industry, attending a fascinating lecture afterward. And Baz had not made Randi feel provincial or geeky for being so awed by the display of Roman history.

They'd attended a piano performance at the Arlene Schnitzer Concert Hall that had moved Randi to tears. Baz had gently teased her while offering his handkerchief, but he'd enjoyed it, too, making not a single comparison to other great soloists he'd heard.

Today she was getting off early so they could go to the zoo. There was a baby elephant that she couldn't wait to see.

And she had her own good news in regard to the babies. She'd peed on the stick that morning and discovered she was not pregnant. While she'd felt a tiny sliver of disappointment, it was overridden by profound relief. Randi wasn't ready for parenthood.

And as much as she wished she could keep Baz in her life, she knew that wasn't realistic. Nor did she want the only reason they had to communicate to be a child they had together.

She had no fantasies—okay, none that she would admit to—that he'd want something more permanent with her if a child was in the mix. Baz was eminently practical. If he offered to help her raise the baby, he would do it, but that didn't mean he and she would have a relationship.

So baby elephants would be plenty of cuteness for them to share before he went back to Spain.

No matter what her heart might want.

She'd done her best to ignore its leanings, but

had been no more successful than trying not to look forward to their time together with abject enthusiasm.

Randi was falling in love. The most terrifying thing about it was that her feelings were a hundred times stronger than they'd been for the almost fiancé. Which meant when Baz did go back to Spain and never called again, she'd be looking a tsunami of pain right in the face.

And there was nothing she could do to stop it.

Her heart was already engaged and it was a stubborn organ.

Interrupting her hopeless thoughts, Baz came through her open office door in the most casual outfit she'd seen to date. His slacks still looked tailored, but he was wearing an expensive-looking dark blue sweater over a black T-shirt, his coat a sleek leather jacket with an off-center zip. He looked hot and modern, when she knew in many ways he was anything but.

"You ready for the zoo?" she asked, trying to ignore the way her heart rate increased the second she saw him.

"You are sure you wouldn't rather go to the Portland Art Museum? I've read they have an impressive selection on exhibit."

She laughed, not in the least deterred. "Nope. Baby elephants. What could be cuter?"

"Baby people?"

"You don't sound too sure."

"I missed most of my nephew and niece's baby-hoods." The chagrin in his expression and tone let her know he regretted that.

"Too busy bringing Perez Holdings back from the brink?" She stood up from her desk and grabbed her purse and jacket.

"*Sí.*"

"There will be other babies in the family," she comforted. Maybe even his own. Though not with her. Dismissing the depressing thought, she opined, "I'm pretty much of the opinion that if it's a baby, it's going to be adorable. People or animal."

"Even baby snakes?"

She shivered. He had to go there? "Okay, no. I'm not a reptile fan."

"You realize that's speciesism?"

"Is that even a word?"

"It is."

"Doesn't matter. I don't want to see baby reptiles, of any kind." Okay, maybe baby turtles. But that was it.

"Lizards can be quite fascinating." He looked like he was laughing at her.

She didn't care. "You can visit that area of the zoo on your own."

He gave her a pirate's grin. "Oh, I think not. If I'm visiting the zoo, you are coming to every habitat with me."

"Not a chance." It didn't matter how many people loved snakes and lizards. More power to them, but Randi was not in their group.

He stepped away from the door to help her into her jacket. "We'll see."

"Not if we don't get there soon, we won't," she said as he gently lifted her hair from beneath the coat's collar.

The baby elephant was every bit as darling as Randi thought it would be, but even more enchanting was how fascinated Baz behaved by every single animal they saw. The billionaire acted like he'd never seen an animal, any animal, up close. She couldn't wait until they got to the interactive exhibit.

"How long since the last time you were at the zoo?" she asked outside the elephant enclosure.

He waved at a zookeeper and the woman nodded. "I've never been."

Randi wondered what that was about.

"Not even when you were little?" she asked, too surprised by Baz's admission to focus on the odd interaction with the zookeeper. While she'd never been, she knew that Spain boasted a couple of phenomenal zoos and several aquariums of note. "What about aquariums?"

"No." Maybe he hadn't lived near any of them.

Though surely his father would have taken a trip to give the experience to the only son that lived with him. "But..." It just seemed so wrong. "What did you do as a child?"

"I learned to live without my mother, and how to live with the new women in my father's life."

Okay, that was not what she meant, but it was some major insight into how Baz saw his own childhood. "You said you and your father were close."

"I said he was a good father and a more hands-on parent than my mother, but he was running a multinational company. No time for trips to the park, the zoo or the like. No time for pets, either."

Appalled, but doing her best to hide it, Randi said, "If he was that dedicated to the company, I'm surprised it was doing so badly when you took over."

"He made some bad decisions. He was too emotionally invested in properties that lost income, too focused on the women in his life to always see when the business needed more attention."

That didn't sound like a father who had much attention left over for his son. Baz's loyalty to his family was even more laudable considering how he'd actually been raised.

"You don't suffer the same weaknesses."

"No, I do not."

"Seriously, though. What did you do for fun as a child?" Okay, he didn't visit a zoo, but he had to have played and spent time with his father in some way to have such a good opinion of his parenting.

"I had toys, playmates."

"What did your dad do with you?"

Baz paused for a moment. "He taught me history by taking me to the places history was made. He taught me to enjoy museums and art galleries."

"As a child?" she asked, a little disbelieving.

"He never treated me like I could not understand the value of what was on display. He told me stories that made the exhibits and the art I was looking at interesting. *Papá* took me to work with him from the time I was a small child, letting me play in his office, though I'm sure that wasn't conducive to doing business. And he taught me to sail." The warmth that memory brought out in Baz was obvious in his tone and the darkening of his espresso eyes.

"Um…sure, that sounds fun." She was not a huge fan of boats. It wasn't a rational fear, but after her mom tried to drown her in the bath when she was six, big bodies of water gave Randi nightmares.

It didn't have to make sense; it just was.

Baz laughed. "I enjoyed it."

"Do you still sail?"

"Not often, but when I need silence, to be away from the constant demands on my time."

She'd noticed how many texts and calls he got. He didn't answer them all, but Baz kept his finger on the pulse of his company. While he never picked up the phone during sex, she'd heard him on the phone in the middle of the night more than once, and he'd rolled over to text something in the dark.

Randi instinctively knew it was business, and when she let him know she was awake, Baz often told her whatever the issue, question or update had been. She liked that he didn't make her ask. The few words she overheard confirmed the business nature of his calls.

Besides, she'd done an internet searching on Baz and found out that he'd broken up with his latest girlfriend several months before. None of the gorgeous, sleek companions in between were seen on his arm more than once, so she believed when he said he wasn't with anyone else.

"Does your father still sail with you?"

He smiled, as if at a fond memory. "At least twice a year. We skipper a boat in the Christmas Regatta and at least one summer regatta each year."

"That sounds fun," she said a little wistfully.

If nothing else, she'd love to see the side of Basilio Perez that came out when he was skippering a boat on the open water. She was sure it was something few ever got to know.

"We both enjoy it," he confirmed. "How about you, *mi hermosa*? Do you sail?"

Randi shook her head, maybe a little too vehemently. "I'm not fond of boats." Or the bodies of water they floated on.

"Really?" His dark brows drew together in confusion, like he couldn't imagine such a thing.

"Oh, yes. Really." She was definite. As much

as she'd like to see the relaxed Baz who got away from it all, she would never be able to climb on board the boat. She didn't even like walking on the docks that jutted out into the water. "I prefer my feet on dry ground."

"Boats are not wet." There was laughter in his voice as he informed her, "They float above the water, not under it."

"If you're lucky."

"Are you afraid of water?"

"Of course not. You've seen me in the bath." Not that she'd taken as many baths in the past two years as she had since meeting him. She preferred showers. Only she never got that sinking feeling when she was with him, and relaxing into the hot water had become something pleasurable.

Something it had not been since she was six.

"That's not what I'm talking about."

"I thought we were talking about baby elephants."

A zookeeper came up to them. "We're ready for you now."

Baz turned a brilliant smile on Randi. "Speaking of, would you like to meet her up close?"

"You're not serious." Randi looked between him and the zookeeper.

Both stared back expectantly.

"You are serious!" Randi exclaimed, still not quite believing Baz had set this up. "We can go into the enclosure?" With all the elephants?

"Not quite. We have the baby in the indoor area." The zookeeper led the way to a huge enclosure fit with numerous skylights. The baby elephant was playing with a large red ball near a tree with many branches.

"The rest of the elephants are outside." The zookeeper turned to Baz. "They told you we have to keep the visit short, right? She's still young enough that keeping her from her mom for very long is not a great idea."

"That is fine."

Randi looked up at Baz. "How did you manage this?"

"With the help of my very efficient executive assistant and a large donation to the pachyderm program here at the zoo."

They got to spend about fifteen minutes with the baby elephant, petting the bristly hair on its head and watching her play.

"She seems to like your hair," Baz teased as the baby elephant ruffled through Randi's shoulder-length brown hair for the second time. "She wants to pet you, too."

"Maybe it's the tea tree oil in my shampoo." Elephants ate leaves, so that made sense to Randi.

"It could be," the zookeeper agreed with a smile.

"Or maybe she just likes you," Baz offered.

Too quickly, they were exiting the inner enclosure after thanking the keeper for allowing them the visit.

Randi couldn't help asking how much Baz had donated to make their time with the baby elephant possible. When he told her, her knees went a little weak. "Wow, um…okay. I can't imagine spending that on a weekend date, much less fifteen minutes."

Baz shrugged as they walked toward the next animal habitat. "It made you happy. And she was as charming as you implied she would be."

"Well, I'm glad you are enjoying yourself. You certainly went out of your way to make sure this will be *the* zoo visit I always remember."

"I'm glad. And I am enjoying myself a lot more than I expected to." If he sounded a little shocked by the fact, she wasn't going to take offense.

They spent another hour at the zoo before driving downtown for dinner. Baz was solicitous and attentive at the tiny but exclusive restaurant that served Asian fusion food, encouraging Randi to try dishes she hadn't before, and comparing the American version of the food to that which he would have found in Madrid.

He wasn't critical, merely urbane in his observations.

"I'd love to visit Spain someday," she admitted.

His lips turned down for a second, his eyes revealing some kind of regret before his face went neutral again. "Perhaps you will."

"Maybe." But not with him. That was a given. And if not with him, would visiting his homeland cause too many painful memories? Probably.

After dinner he drove toward his own executive condo, rather than her apartment as they had agreed outside the restaurant. "So, the art museum tomorrow?"

"I can't," she said with genuine regret. "I'm going shopping with Kayla to find an outfit to wear for my television interview."

"Skip the interview and you can spend the evening with me," he offered beguilingly.

"You know I can't do that." But a giant part of Randi wished she could.

"No, I do not know that." He pulled the car to a

stop at a red light and turned to look at her, his expression serious. "This interview is going to bring much more pain into your life than the good you imagine it will."

"You can't know that."

"I assure you, I can. Which of us has more experience with the media?"

"I have plenty experience." All of it awful. She was ready to have the truth about her out there. She needed it.

Only the idea of the interview? Terrified her. And what could happen afterward? He was right. It could turn her life into another circus where she was performing the high-wire act on a greased rope without a safety net. But like Kayla had said, Randi had to do *something*.

Both women had agreed they'd had their fill of being victims in their own lives.

"No. You have been attacked, hurt and victimized by the media." His tone was implacable as he pulled away from the light. "You believe that will change when you get your side of the story out."

"You don't, though?" Why didn't he?

It would help her if Andreas was all for the interview, but it was Kayla who understood Randi's need to act, to fight back, and had pushed for Randi to get her side of the story out in such a way. Andreas had warned them both doing the spot could boomerang back on Randi, bringing the crazies out of the woodwork as well as the critics that would never be swayed by the truth.

Both men, who had a clearly more cynical view of humanity than the sisters, had expressed caution about Randi telling her story in such a way.

"No." In profile, Baz's jaw looked hewn from granite. "I believe if you keep this story going, while you are bound to find supporters, you will end up on the receiving end of more hate and cruelty. It's unlikely anyone who has written about you in the past will reverse their stand."

"How can you be so sure of that?"

"Tell me this. Do you think the Madisons will sit back and accept your version of events?" Baz asked, rather than answered. Maybe his question was the answer.

"But I have proof." The same proof she'd refused to go public with five years ago out of compassion for what the family was already going through.

"And they have a PR machine. You said so yourself."

"This time I have someone on my side who will help me fight back." More than one someone. She had her sister. She had Andreas. And Randi's father and grandparents had always stood up with her.

They just hadn't had the power and influence to do it with any real effect.

"You cannot expect that of me." Baz sounded almost panicked, or as panicked as Mr. Cool-Shark-Businessman was likely to get. "I will not be in Portland indefinitely."

"I wasn't talking about you." But now she knew that he would not be one of the people in her corner. And that was fine.

She hadn't expected anything else. Not really. Hope? Well, that was a drug she knew better than to indulge in.

"Andreas?" Baz asked.

"Yes." Among others. "He's my brother by marriage and he told me I'm the family he chose. He's big on loyalty to family that deserves it, like his wife and me."

"He can't prevent the internet trolls from coming out of the woodwork, or the less scrupulous paparazzi from hunting you down."

"Maybe they'll attack the Madisons this time."

"Is that what you really want?"

No, but… "They deserve it! They destroyed my life."

"The parents, maybe. But the children?" Baz pressed on with that ruthlessness he'd warned her about. "Do you want little Jamie attacked at school because of something his mother did? Isn't it bad enough he has a mother who could neglect him so shamefully?"

"I… Look… It's not…" It was no good. Randi had been ignoring the impact her interview might have on the Madisons' children on purpose. Knowing if she thought about it, she'd never be able to go through with the interview. "I don't want to hurt Jamie, or his sister."

"Then you cannot do the interview."

"But what about me?" she asked painfully. "What about *my* life? *My* family? It's started all over again already. I'm getting awful things posted about me online, news articles full of lies written about the incident five years ago. I can't just move away and change my name again. There's too much interest in Andreas and Kayla. There will always be a reporter interested in the story if I don't tell my side."

"If you tell your side, you'll cause a furor of interest, and the story will live much longer with the truth of Tiffany's shameful neglect. There is another option, you know?"

"No, I don't know."

"We can change the story entirely. What if I could convince the Madisons to not only sign a gag order for future commentary on the incident, but also to issue a press release saying they have never blamed you for the tragic, *unavoidable* accident? If I could ensure their PR machine would not only leave you alone, but also turn their attention toward presenting you in a positive light? Would that work for you? Would it give you what you need?"

"You would do that?" She thought his comment about going back to Spain meant Baz had no interest in getting involved. In any way. "Why would you do that?"

His knuckles turned white from Baz's grip on the steering wheel. "Because I do not want you to end up more hurt than you already have been."

Hope blossomed, but then collapsed under reality. "It won't work. Andreas already tried to reason with Mr. Madison. It didn't go well."

Which was an understatement.

"Mr. Madison owes you an apology."

"That's what Andreas said."

"I will make sure you get it. Andreas is good at what he does, but he does not have my experience dealing with situations like this."

"You have experience with situations like this?" she asked with disbelief.

"Not exactly, but I have three stepmothers and another one about to marry my father. I have learned how to deal with unreasonable and entitled people, getting them to rein in their expectations."

"You really think you can convince that man to say he's sorry?" Much less the rest of it.

"I think I can do more than that. I can get a sizable donation for Kayla's for Kids, a press release from him and his wife deeply regretting the continued media interest in their old tragedy and the gag order I mentioned, naturally."

He was serious. He really meant it. Baz would use his considerable power and influence to right a wrong that had plagued Randi's life for five long years. Nothing could undo the trauma she'd endured hitting a child with her car. She hadn't been able to drive for two years afterward, but if he could stop the piranhas from circling, that would be amazing.

Relief poured through Randi and she realized in

that moment how much she truly hadn't wanted to do the interview. "If you think it will work, I'll do it."

"You'll cancel the interview?" He sounded relieved all out of proportion.

Maybe he did care. At least a little.

"*After* I get an apology, the press release goes out and they sign the gag order." She wasn't a complete pushover, no matter how much she didn't want to see Jamie and his sister forced to deal with the aftermath of the interview.

"Give me twenty-four hours."

He thought he could get it accomplished that quickly? She only hoped Baz was right. "I can't believe you're doing this for me."

"Why wouldn't I?"

She didn't have an answer for him, other than the fact that they had sex, not a relationship. "Are you always this helpful to women you date casually?" she asked by way of an answer.

"What we have is—" He stopped abruptly, looking startled by what he was about to say. Baz cleared his throat. "Casual, yes, but that does not mean I cannot do this small thing for you."

"Trust me. Dealing with Carl Madison is not a small thing."

"For you, maybe. For me? *Sí, lo es*."

Yes, it is, she internally translated and smiled. "For a corporate mega shark, you sure have a white-knight complex going on."

He grimaced. "I assure you, I am no white knight."

Her smile did not dim. It was kind of sweet how he didn't want her to think he was *that* guy when he so obviously was.

The executive condo he was staying in was in a multistory brick building on one of the pretty tree-lined streets near the downtown center. Baz pulled his luxury rental into the secure underground parking garage after the liveried attendant opened the gate for them.

Even the elevator up to his floor was swank, the walls paneled in light wood; no flyers for upcoming local events pasted to these walls.

Though there was a brass plaque informing residents that the concierge would be happy to help them find entertainment or dining options as well as anything else they might require.

A condo complex with a concierge? Now, that was upscale.

They took the elevator to the top floor. Of course. The doors swished open to an elegant but modern foyer, a square settee on one wall, a console table flanked by two chairs and topped with a vase of lilies on the opposite. Everything in shades of creams and browns, it had a peaceful vibe and she could imagine visitors for the residents waiting here comfortably. Four corridors led off from the space to what she assumed were entrances to each corner penthouse apartment.

"Finally!" A demanding and oddly familiar voice shattered the peace of the space. "Where the hell have you been? You haven't answered any of my calls, Baz. That is not acceptable."

Although she couldn't yet see the man, standing as she was on the other side of Baz, Randi now recognized the voice coming from the corridor on their right and it sent ice through her veins.

Carl Madison.

CHAPTER SEVEN

WHAT IN THE world was Carl Madison doing here and why was he berating Baz? Had Randi's temporary lover already instigated talks on her behalf with the awful man?

And why did he think he could call Basilio by the more familiar nickname, Baz?

"Carl, what the hell are you doing here?" Baz asked with undisguised fury.

So, not friends, then, but they were on a first-name basis. How did that work? What was going on? Why would Mr. Madison have come to Baz's penthouse?

"If you answered your damn phone I would not have had to track you down," Mr. Madison said, sounding both annoyed and aggrieved. "That bitch is going to do that interview in two weeks. The station is already doing internet promotion for the spot, alluding to a brand-new revelation of *document-supported facts*. What are you doing about it?"

"Hell, Carlos. *Eres un idiota!*" Baz lunged away from Randi toward the man he'd just called Carlos. Not Carl. He grabbed Mr. Madison by the lapels of his jacket and jerked him forward. *"No usarás un lenguaje como ese sobre o alrededor de Miranda."*

Baz's explosion into motion had shocked her, but the fury in his tone as he demanded the other man not use that kind of language about or around her made her feel a little better in a situation she did not understand.

"Speak English." Mr. Madison was trying to break Baz's hold on his jacket to no avail. "You're in America, little brother."

"Little brother?" Randi asked, absolutely not wanting to believe the implication of what she was hearing, but unable to ignore the evidence of her eyes and ears.

Mr. Madison jerked at the sound of her voice, looking past his brother to meet Randi's bewildered gaze. Surprise and consternation crossed his face before it settled into lines of straight-out annoyance.

"Oh, hell. Why did you bring her here?" Mr. Madison demanded as Baz moved to block the older man's line of sight to her. "I guess it's out of the bag now. Not that you were making progress." Oh, the disgust just dripped from Carl Madison's voice.

But *progress*? What exactly was out of the bag? Randi gave herself a mental shake, reminding herself she was no doe-eyed optimist. If it walked like a duck, it was going to quack.

Basilio Perez was Carl…no, *Carlos* Madison's brother. All the clues had been there. The siblings whose mother had taken them to raise in another country, even giving them the last name of her second husband. Carl Madison had been born Carlos Perez.

And he was a member of the family Baz had been so clear he owed all his loyalty to, one of the people Baz had made it clear he was willing to be downright merciless on behalf of.

Never had Randi been so tempted to use a certain four-letter expletive. Not even when the toerag trying to peer around his brother to glare at her had hit and threatened her.

"All of this was about you convincing me not to do the interview," she accused Baz's back.

His big body stiffened. Then his brother dropped against the wall, stumbling to his knees, as Baz spun to face Randi. "I told you why I do not want you to do the interview."

She almost bought his distress, but she couldn't afford to spend that kind of emotional currency.

"You lied to me." She couldn't have hidden the pain that knowledge caused her, so she didn't try.

"I told you I was no white knight."

"You think that makes it okay?" she cried. This could not be real.

The first man in years she'd shared her body with had been using her just like the last one. Her heart felt like it was exploding in her chest, detonating from the pain expanding inside her.

"Nothing has changed from five minutes ago. Yes, I regret to say that sorry excuse for humanity is my older brother, but he was not in our bed with us."

"You had sex with her to get her to call off the interview? You do have a ruthless streak, don't you?" Mr. Madison sounded like he was impressed.

Randi just wanted to throw up.

Baz spun back to the older man and got right into his face, in a move more emotional than orchestrated. "Shut up. This has nothing to do with you."

"Like hell," Mr. Madison barked.

"Of course it does," Randi said painfully at the same time.

She understood why Baz was so upset. His brother's impatience had undone all of Basilio Perez's efforts in, and out of, the bedroom. He'd had her, too. She'd been on the verge of doing exactly what the brothers wanted.

Baz turned back, stepping toward her. "No, it really does not. Carlos has treated you shamefully. I still want to fix that."

"How is deceiving and using me going to fix anything?" For her anyway.

She could see what his agenda had been on behalf of his family easily enough, but no way did that translate into making things better for her.

He opened his mouth to speak, but seemed unsure what to say. Randi doubted very much that the great Basilio Perez often found himself lost for words.

She put her hand up, forestalling whatever his facile brain was coming up with. "I can't believe anything you say." He'd been dishonest with her from the start. "You orchestrated our meeting, didn't you?"

His jaw clenched, but he nodded. "I did."

"You lied about everything!"

"Actually, I lied about very little." He stepped closer to her and she moved back, maintaining their distance. He frowned, but stopped. "The only thing I withheld from you was the name of my family here."

"You knew I would never suspect you of being related to the people who had destroyed my life. The times we talked about the accident, you deliberately pretended not to know anything about it." How was pretense not a lie?

"We destroyed your life?" Mr. Madison was apparently done being ignored. "You put our son in a coma for two weeks!"

"I never denied driving the car, but I *wasn't* speeding. I *wasn't* driving negligently. Jamie ran out from between parked cars, right in front of my bumper. I did my best to avoid him. If I hadn't, things would have been so much worse. I know the doctors told you that." Because they'd told her when she'd inquired about the little boy's state of health.

The entire situation had been beyond devastating. One of the reasons she hadn't fought back against all the criticism, despite the proof she had access to that showed so much of what was said about her was a total fabrication, was because she'd felt a horrific guilt. Deserved or not, Randi had never completely gotten over the moment of impact between her car and that tiny body. She probably never would.

Mr. Madison dismissed Randi's words with some ugly language, but no actual argument to the contrary.

Baz pointed at his brother, his expression bordering on fury. "The accident was unavoidable once *your wife* let your four-year-old son wander off toward a busy street."

"Is that what that bitch told you?"

Baz moved so fast, Randi gasped. But he had his brother up by his collar again and spoke right into his face. "I told you not to call her that!"

Mr. Madison's face turned red, his nasty expression in no way diminished. "Remember who your family is here, Baz!"

"Right now I'm ashamed of the connection."

"How dare you say that?"

"How dare *you* hit a defenseless woman?"

Randi wasn't exactly defenseless, but she agreed the jerk should never have gotten physical with her. She wished he'd just forget she existed.

"That bitch is not defenseless!"

"I warned you!" Baz cocked his arm and then punched his brother, right in the face, before throwing him toward the wall. "How does that feel?"

Mr. Madison swiped at his now-bleeding nose. "I can't believe you hit me!"

"We are of a size." He indicated Randi with his hand. "She, however, is nowhere near your weight class. And. You. Hit. Her."

"I told you things got out of hand. I shouldn't have done that."

"That is not good enough." Baz seemed to pull his cool in around him, his voice turning more frigid than a Midwest winter. "You will keep a civil tongue in your head or I will knock out every one of your capped teeth."

Cautiously eyeing his younger brother, Mr. Madison pushed himself up the wall. "Okay, I get it. You're protective, though Heaven only knows why."

Protective? Right. Not so much from where Randi was standing.

Betrayal was flaying her with the sting of twenty lashes. "Sex between us…it was all about you seducing me into doing what you wanted."

And man, but she did not want to discuss this in front of Carl Madison.

Baz held himself rigidly, but took several seconds to come back around to face her. He reached toward her again.

But she stepped back farther, hitting the wall, unable to bear the idea of even the most casual touch. "Just admit it. Don't keep lying."

"I told you. I didn't actually lie to you."

"You deceived me and that isn't going away on a technicality. Do you honestly think I would have spent five minutes, let alone five days, in your company if I knew who you were related to?" One thing was for sure—she wasn't compounding that mistake. "No wonder you stood up for people I thought were strangers to you. They were part of the family you are so willing to protect at all costs!"

"But I saw your side, as well. You know I did. Carlos knows I did. I am certain that is one of the reasons he so stupidly showed up here today. He knew I was not interested in protecting him and Tiffany if it meant more of the same intimidation tactics and lies."

Didn't that sound nice? But it didn't in any way mitigate the truth. "You had sex with me as a ploy!"

"I—"

"Don't you dare try to deceive me again. At least be honest about it now," she practically begged him.

His head dropped, his pride draining away if she believed it. "I did. But—"

"No, no *buts*, no excuses." Hearing the confirmation didn't make her feel any better. "At least you're being honest. Finally."

"I will not lie to you."

She laughed, the sound harsh and unnatural, coming from her. "Like I believe you."

"You have my word."

"Which is worth nothing. According to you, you never actually told me anything untrue in the first place. Only that doesn't make one second of your underhanded behavior any better. Why can't you see that?"

"My deception was not meant to harm you."

"You're so used to getting your way, you don't care what means you use to do it. Just like your brother." She glared at Carl Madison, who watched her and his brother like a spectator at a tennis match. "The final joke is on you. Your male Mata Hari had convinced me to cancel the interview on the way over."

"That's great!" Suddenly Mr. Madison was all smiles, despite his rumpled clothes and bloody face. "You'll be glad you did."

The threat was there in his tone and it firmed her resolve. "I said the joke was on you because you being here, showing me what Baz… Basilio's real game was, it changed my mind. I'm doing that interview, but I won't just be talking about what happened five years ago. I'm telling the world how you convinced your brother to prostitute himself for you. I'm showing pictures of my face after you hit me. I'm telling the network about the assault charges I leveled against you and how you've broken the restraining order. You think you've got all the cards? You think you can ruin my life again? Think again! I may not have a white knight in my corner, but I have a family, and they are as loyal to me as he is to you. Only they aren't underhanded and sneaky about it. You'll see the attack coming, but you still won't be able to defend yourselves!"

With that she spun and jabbed the elevator button. She was leaving. She couldn't stand another second in those two men's company.

She saw the elevator doors open through the blur of angry tears. Grateful it had still been on their floor, she stepped into it.

Baz slipped in with her. "Miranda, please look at me."

"Go to hell." She couldn't look at him. It hurt too much.

"I did not mean to hurt you."

She looked at him then, too shocked at his stupidity. "What did you think was going to happen?"

"I thought I would tell you the truth on my own terms."

"So you admit there was a truth to tell?" Saying he hadn't actually lied to her!

"A revelation to be made, definitely."

"You hid your connection to the Madisons from me."

"I did."

"So?"

"'So I think we have something special."

"Are you kidding me? We don't have *anything* real."

"You don't mean that." His confidence was misplaced.

She lifted her gaze to his, not caring if he saw the devastation in hers. "How could I mean anything else? Don't you realize how deeply you've betrayed me?"

His dark eyes widened, like the idea shocked him. "That was not my intention."

"Really? You knew exactly what you were doing when you seduced me in hopes of using our sexual relationship to influence me into doing what you want."

"Surely the seduction was mutual."

"Don't be any more of an ass than you have to!"

"I know you are angry—"

"You think?"

He made an aborted movement with his hands, dropping them to his sides, like he remembered she didn't want him touching her. "But once you've had time to think, you will realize my intentions grew to include protecting you, as well."

"Don't count on it. I've had all the revelations about you I'm going to." She glared into his espresso gaze, so there could be no question she meant what she said. "I never want to see anyone from your blighted family again in my lifetime and that's the only reason I'm not filing a civil suit against all of you!"

"You don't mean that."

Could he really be that dense? "Oh, yes, I really do."

"What about the baby?"

She wanted to scream at him for even asking that question, but she instead gritted out, "There is no baby."

"We could work on that." His tone and expression didn't suggest he was kidding.

All the air whooshed from her lungs. "You... That's..."

"We're good together, better than good. We connect in a way I have never experienced with another woman."

The elevator reached the ground floor and she stepped out. "Connect with this!" For the first time in her life, Randi flipped someone off.

She stormed toward the doors to the street.

Ignoring her clear desire to be rid of him, Baz followed. "I'll drive you home."

"Not a chance."

"Let me call a taxi for you at least."

"I can call my own darn Uber if I want one." A ride on the MAX, lost in the crowd of Portlanders, sounded good right now, though.

She shoved open the lobby doors and stepped onto the street. Rain poured down, but she didn't care. Like Kayla said often enough, she might be sweet, but she wasn't made of sugar; she wasn't going to melt in a little Oregon liquid sunshine.

Baz followed her as she hiked it to the nearest MAX station. If she remembered correctly, it was about ten blocks down and over.

"Please, Miranda. You do not need to go off like this."

She spun to face him, rain running in rivulets down her face. "Can't you leave me alone? Your plan failed. Deal with it."

"You are going to catch your death in this rain." He stripped off his leather jacket and held it over her head, while he grew increasingly soaked.

"I'll be fine! It's not your problem."

"You should stand under an awning while you call and wait for your driver." He indicated an awning-covered doorway to their left with his head.

She shook hers. "I'm taking the train."

"Alone?" Shock at the idea infused that single word until it was a full statement.

"I don't need an escort." To prove it, she walked away from the shelter of his coat and off down the street. "I've been riding public transportation on my own for a very long time."

"That cannot be safe!" His words proved he followed her as she'd suspected he would.

Basilio Perez wasn't just pitiless about achieving

his own objectives, but the man gave new definition to the word *stubborn*.

"Oh, get out of your gold-plated tower," she threw over her shoulder. "Those of us not in your tax bracket use public transportation all the time."

"You have your own car."

"That doesn't mean I don't know how to take a bus or a train."

"I think you would argue with me about anything right now."

Tears mixed with the rain on her cheeks. "Okay, maybe you're not completely stupid."

"I will walk you to the MAX station." He had managed to maneuver his coat over her head again, like a moving awning as he stayed in step with her.

"Can't you take a hint? I don't want to see you."

"Then do not look behind you." He allowed his body to move to her rear while still keeping the protection over her from the rain.

"Why are you so stubborn?"

"Being anything less would never serve me."

She shook her head. "Do you know how close to hating you I am?"

He said nothing, but there was an air about him, like her words surprised him. Did he really expect her to keep admiring him after what she'd learned?

Unwilling to ponder his feelings or thoughts any longer, she increased her pace toward the MAX station in the cold rain.

True to his word, Baz followed her but kept behind her, out of her line of sight. She did her best to ignore the sense of safety his presence gave her, or how wet and cold he must be getting while protecting her from the downpour.

When they reached the platform, she bought a ticket with her phonc and then gasped in outrage when she noticed Baz doing the same thing.

"Seriously, Mr. Perez, you need to go away!"

"I'm not comfortable with you riding the train alone."

"Don't be such a control freak. I'm safer on the train than I was around your brother. Maybe even you."

"What is that supposed to mean? I would never physically harm you."

"You punched your own brother!"

"If you had not been there, I probably would have done more." And Baz didn't look in the least repentant about that fact. "He deserved a dose of his own temper."

"Just like your family to resort to violence when things don't go your way." Guilt assailed her as the words left her mouth.

She didn't believe them, and Baz had been defending her when he hit his brother. It wasn't lost on her that Baz had meted out exactly what had been done to her by Carl Madison and his bodyguard.

"When you get to know me better, you will realize how untrue that statement is."

"I'm not going to get to know you better."

Baz didn't reply, simply looked up as the train came into the station.

He took a seat behind her after giving the one beside her a considering look. Her glare must have told him what a bad idea sitting there would be.

She spent the ride trying to ignore his presence and swallow back the tears that just did not want to go away. She also called her sister to see if she or Andreas could pick Randi up from the MAX stop closest to her apartment. Otherwise, it would have been a couple-mile walk to her apartment from there, with no nearby buses that could shorten it.

Kayla said of course she'd be there and then asked what was wrong.

"I'll tell you when you pick me up," Randi promised, unwilling to get into it in front of Baz, much less all the strangers on the train.

Basilio watched Miranda climb into her sister's car with frustration. He did not understand his own actions. *Sí*, he was still committed to protecting the young ones of his family, but following her onto the train?

He had used her safety as the excuse for doing so, but he'd known it was more. He could not stand to let Miranda walk away without another word, without trying to make her understand. Not that he'd gotten the chance to do that. And still, he'd been glad to sit behind her on the MAX, to simply stay near.

Cracks were forming in his formidable defenses around his innermost emotions. He did not like it, but if she called right that minute, he would have the driver turn the car around without hesitation to be with her.

If only Carlos had not screwed everything up so spectacularly.

His brother was truly the *idiota* Basilio had called him. Carlos's impatience had cost them any chance of Miranda backing out of the interview and so he told the older man when he found him *inside* his penthouse when Basilio returned.

He'd called for a car with no shame. He'd been soaked through and had no intention of waiting around for a train to take him back to the stop he'd gotten on, only to be followed by another walk in the rain.

"How was I supposed to know you'd bring the little tar—" Carlos broke off at Basilio's look. "That woman here?"

"Why would I not bring her here?" Basilio walked into his bedroom without waiting for an answer and stripped out of his wet clothes.

His brother yelled from the other room, "Because she's the enemy!"

Basilio donned fresh slacks and a black cashmere turtleneck before rejoining his brother. "Miranda is not my enemy. She was as much a victim five years ago as Jamie. If anyone was at fault for that tragedy, it was Tiffany." Basilio held up his hand to forestall his brother's denial. "And now because of your impatience and lack of trust in me, millions of morning show viewers will learn that truth."

Not to mention other facts that would stir up

plenty of scandal for both the Madison and Perez names.

"You have to stop her!"

"How? She despises me now." But didn't quite hate him. That knowledge had shocked Basilio, but also given him some measure of hope.

"Threaten her, threaten her brother-in-law's company."

"You assume I have the power to do that?"

"You know you do."

"But I have no desire to. Now that I know the truth of the circumstances, all threats toward Miranda and her family are off the table."

"*We're* still your family."

"Only when it is convenient for you." And the connection was becoming less and less advantageous to Basilio.

"Don't whine."

"I'm hardly doing that, simply pointing out that you can't play the family card and expect me to ignore how often you forget I'm your brother."

"Our father would expect you to help me."

"Our father would be appalled to realize you remained married to a woman who put your son so firmly in harm's way."

"Just because the man doesn't understand marital fidelity and commitment doesn't mean I don't. Tiffany is my wife and I love her."

"While that sentiment is creditable, you know how little regard I have for that emotion as an excuse for inexcusable behavior." He gave Carlos a long, unfriendly look his brother would do well to take heed of. "Be very careful how you speak of a man who is truly *mi familia*."

"He divorced your mother, too."

Basilio just stared at his brother until the older man squirmed in his seat. "Remember that your company owes a lot of its success to the connection you have with Perez Holdings. Respect those connections *in every way*, or lose them. In. Every. Way."

He was done playing happy families with Carlos. The man might have done what he had in order to protect his own wife, but that did not change the fact that his behavior had been completely lacking in honor or integrity. It was one thing to do what needed to be done, another entirely to completely lose sight of one's moral compass while doing so.

It was Basilio's hope that once Miranda had calmed down, she would realize that while he might be ruthless, he was never without honor.

"You're threatening me?" Carlos demanded with

a sneer. "Armand would never let you withdraw support from your brother's company."

"*Mi papá* no longer owns even a nominal interest in the company."

"But he's still a director."

"Because I will it to be so."

"You took the family company from our father."

"I took over the bankrupt company, yes, and I brought it forth new from the ashes of poor decisions and debt. Perez Holdings is *my* company and any decision I make stands as *Papá* and all of his ex-wives had learned."

"You think you're something so special, lording your billions over us."

Billions that had been nothing but negative numbers when Basilio took the company over ten years earlier. "I think that if you make the mistake of making me your enemy, you will deeply regret it sooner rather than later. And to be clear, if you allow your PR people to continue to attack and spread lies about Miranda Smith, you will in de facto be making me your enemy."

"You don't mean that!"

"When have I ever said something I do not mean?" Basilio had not garnered his reputation bluffing.

Everyone who had done business with him, including his older brother, knew that Basilio never made empty threats. He followed through. Sometimes with overkill. Better to let people see one meant what one said than have them believing you harbored a weakness in one's character.

"Listen closely, Carlos, for what I'm about to say, I will not repeat, nor will I give you a second time to screw up."

"What the hell? Who do you think you are?"

"A man who could burn your company down to the ground if I so desire."

Carlos paled, his belligerent expression suddenly morphing into something Basilio could work with. Fear. "You wouldn't do that. It's my stepfather's company anyway."

CHAPTER EIGHT

"Even less reason for me to care if it is destroyed." And if Carlos did not comprehend that, he was an even bigger fool than Basilio already thought him.

Carlos blustered, "Our father would never do something so underhanded."

"Our father would never have done what you have to Miranda, either. I think we can agree that we are both different from the man who sired us in some very important ways."

"Say what you're going to say."

"You will call your PR dogs off Miranda. In fact, you will give them a new directive. It is your job to repair her reputation as much as it is possible to do."

"That interview she's going to do will take care of that."

Basilio ignored his brother's interruption. "You will craft a formal apology for your assault on her."

"I pushed her. That's not an assault."

"I read the police report and the trial transcript. Both of which are public record. *You* hit her and your bodyguard pushed her down. If you don't want that splashed across the news media with more furor than anything you could ever devise, you will listen."

"More threats?"

"Common decency should be enough to convince you to better behavior, but it is not. Threats will have to suffice, but please remember. I never bluff."

"I know you don't."

"Good." Basilio took a firmer grip on his temper. Never before had he been moved to violence outside his time in the gym, where it was part of training his body. "You will sign a gag order, promising never to comment on the incident of five years ago again, other than to support the story that the Madison family in no way blames, or has ever blamed, Miranda Smith, née Weber, for the tragic but unavoidable accident. You will release a press announcement to that effect, as well."

"No way. If I do that, people are going to start asking why. Someone is going to figure out that Tiffany lost track of Jamie."

"Lost track of would imply she was watching him at all, and evidence is not in her favor."

"I can't let this destroy my family."

"You were happy to destroy Miranda's family."

"We never attacked her father or grandparents."

"Her father had to change schools from the place he'd worked most of his adult life. Her grandparents faced the jackal reporters you set on Miranda. None of this is negotiable, Carlos."

"You know I prefer Carl."

"That matters less than nothing in this moment, but let us be clear. I do not approve of the way you've divorced yourself from our father by taking the name of your stepfather and Americanizing your name. I find your attitude to family and honor contemptible."

Carlos flinched as if struck. "I'm your *older* brother. It is not your job to correct me."

"Someone needs to. Had you and Gracia been allowed to spend time regularly with our father, instead of being raised in America by your mother and stepfather exclusively, perhaps you would not be so entitled and lacking in character."

"You don't need to be so offensive. Our father was the one who had an affair and married his bit on the side."

"That bit on the side was my mother and she suffered the same indignity and yet did not turn that into an excuse for me to live without a conscience."

"I'm sure your business rivals would not say the same."

"Integrity is part and parcel of every deal I've made, no matter how brutal I've had to be in the business arena. You cannot even begin to say the same thing."

"All of this stuff you want me to do for Miranda is going to destroy my family and cause serious issues for the Madison Realty Group."

"You should have considered the fact that there are consequences to every action, good or bad."

"It's your job to help your family."

"And if you hadn't shown up acting like a loudmouthed buffoon, Miranda would have agreed to cancel the interview. Now she's set to let us all crash and burn."

"And you're going to let that happen? The Perez name is going to be dragged through the mud, too, and we both know how important that is to you."

"I am aware." He had to hope that once her temper had cooled some, Miranda might consider her actions and the impact they would have on Jamie and Grace. "She won't back down on my behalf, or even yours, but Miranda has more compassion in her tiny finger than you and the entire Madison family has in its collective body."

Carlos looked at him wonderingly. "You've fallen for the little gold digger."

"Excuse me?" He didn't care about the accusation that he'd fallen for Miranda, but no way in hell was he tolerating more name-calling on her behalf.

An *aha* expression crossed Carlos's features. "I mean Miranda."

"She is no gold digger. She never had any expectation of a lasting relationship with me." Only now did he realize, after she'd walked away from him with such finality, that perhaps he wished she did.

"She's a saint," Carlos said, his voice laced with sarcasm.

"*Es verdad*, she is something very special."

"You *have* fallen for her!"

"I never denied it."

"Never mind what she's set to do to our family, which apparently you no longer care about, but you can't have a relationship with a woman like that! You could do so much better."

"There is no better."

"You cannot be serious."

"You think not? When have you known me to joke?"

"She's a nobody!"

"She's a woman who dedicates her life to the welfare of children. What could be more laudable?"

"That right there should tell you that she feels guilty about what happened to Jamie. That she *is* guilty."

"Don't be more stupid than you can help." Miranda had said something else had sparked her desire to go into social work.

Basilio hoped that there was still a chance she would tell him what that was. Though that hope was slim. Basilio was no quitter, though. And that was something the little spitfire would learn.

"So, even without the promise of her canceling the interview, you want me to basically throw my family under the bus."

"*Si.* If you do, there is a chance, slim as it might be, that she will agree to back out of the morning news show."

"I can't do that, Baz. If you think with your brain and not your dick, you'd realize that."

"I don't care which brain you use. Just use it to

consider what I will do to you and your company if you don't follow through on what I've asked."

"Gracia brought you over to help us, not make things worse."

"Gracia asked for my help on the basis of a series of lies. You are lucky I'm even giving you the choice to take a less damaging path than full disclosure."

"Thank you so much," Carlos said with bitter sarcasm. "When your girlfriend plans to reveal everything anyway."

"That was her hurt and anger talking."

"You think you can seduce her into backing down?" Carlos asked with clear hope.

"I believe her own sense of compassion and concern for others will be enough."

"Now who's being stupid?"

"Still you." Basilio shrugged at his brother's huff of offense. "You asked."

"Tell me at least you're going to try to seduce her again. It worked once. It could work again."

"Oh, I'm going to get her into bed again, but I won't be trying to convince her of anything but accepting me back into her life."

"You're lovestruck! I never would have thought

the great Basilio Perez could be brought down by a mere woman."

"I am in no way brought down." He was the same man he'd always been. The problem here was that his brother had never actually known that man. "If you knew me at all, you would be aware that I do not believe in the concept of romantic love."

Growing up with a father who fell in and out of love so easily and quickly, how could Basilio believe that emotion was anything but a temporary burst of endorphins responsible for some of history's worst decisions, especially the most immediate history of his family?

"And yet you are willing to devastate the family you have never shown anything but loyalty to for the sake of this woman. How is that not love?"

"The fact I will not support the destruction of an innocent life—for the second time, no less—is hardly some kind of proof I believe in fairy tales."

"Whatever you say."

"I hope for your sake that you mean that."

Shaking his head, Carlos stood. "I need to talk to Tiffany."

"I expect to hear from you or a media rep within forty-eight hours."

"You really are a cold bastard, aren't you?"

"So it has been said." Basilio thought of something else he realized needed to be put in place. "You and Tiffany will sign a contract for a visitation schedule for your children with *Papá* and myself in Spain."

"What? What are you talking about?"

"Your children deserve to have adults in their lives who will teach them the meaning of integrity and true family loyalty."

"You can say that after what you are making me do?"

"Without a single doubt, *sí.*"

"You can't force me to give you visitation with my children."

"Can't I?"

Once again, Carlos's naturally olive complexion paled. "Forced visitation isn't going to endear you to them."

"You assume they will not enjoy their time in Spain with a doting grandfather."

"And you? They'll be terrified of you."

"They are not afraid of me now. You will do and say nothing to change that, either. Not if you want continued business connections with the Perez group."

"You're big on the threats."

"They should not be necessary." Basilio allowed every bit of disgust he felt for his brother show in his voice.

The older man winced like he'd gotten the message. "I should have made a bigger effort to be a brother to you. You wouldn't be doing this if I had."

"It's doubtful, but maybe. However, the past is the past and cannot be changed."

"Maybe we could work on being brothers now."

Basilio didn't laugh at his brother's obvious attempt to use the family card again. "Go home and speak to your wife and whoever else you need to. Just remember my deadline."

Carlos frowned when Basilio ignored his overture, but for once he showed some intelligence and left the condo without another word.

Basilio was in no way shocked when he got a phone call from his oldest stepmother. He told her in no uncertain terms what he thought of what had been done to Miranda in the name of protecting Tiffany, as well as the fact Basilio had no intention of backing down from what he had told Carlos. Mrs. Madison tried crying and then shouting at him. When none of her cajoling or threatening worked, she hung up on him.

Thirty minutes later he received a call from his father. This one took more out of Basilio, but he'd learned long ago how to stand up to his father. He could never have saved the company otherwise, much less stop the financial hemorrhaging that was his father's ex-wives.

"So this woman is important enough to you for you to abandon your family."

"She is innocent and does not deserve what was done to her. Had they told me the truth in the beginning, this is the outcome I would have been looking for."

"You think so? You are a ruthless man, Basilio, my son. I do not believe you would have cared nearly so much about the impact your brother's actions had on Miranda's life if you had not come to care for her."

"You know I do not believe in that nonsense."

"Your cynicism toward love is my fault." His father sounded sad about that fact.

"You also taught me what I know about honor and integrity. Do not tell me you approve of the lies Carlos has spread about Miranda, or the way his wife was so grossly neglectful she did not know Jamie had left the park until she heard the sirens and looked up from her phone. How long does it take a four-year-old to wander two city blocks?"

"They have taken measures to make sure such a thing does not happen again."

"Yes, I noticed the way she's never left alone with the children. You don't think she might want simply to change her behavior?"

"Do not judge so harshly. You have never been a parent."

"But you have, and no matter what else you had going on in your life, I was always safe with you."

"Thank you for saying that."

"I'm not going to back off. Carlos knows what he needs to do. I don't suppose he told you that part of my demands was for his children to visit us in Spain regularly."

"No. He did not. You're going to make sure I get to see my grandchildren more than once every couple of years when Carlos allows me to visit?"

"That is the plan, yes. The way Carlos and Gracia grew up without your influence is not something we want repeated in the next generation."

"They are not bad people."

"Just supremely spoiled, self-indulgent and too

comfortable with dishonesty as a means to protect them from facing the consequences of their own actions."

"Were you honest with this young woman when you met her?"

"No, but I never lied outright to her, and I never would have lied about her, causing her hurt."

"You *do* care about her."

Basilio wasn't answering that claim again. He changed the subject and managed to end the call without discussing Miranda any further.

Randi sat next to Kayla on her sofa, each of them eating out of the pint containers of their favorite ice cream flavors. She'd already done the crying bit when Randi told her sister about the whole sorry mess. Now it was time for mindless comfort, or so Kayla claimed.

"You're sure it was all an act?" Kayla asked as Meg Ryan finally admitted her feelings to Billy Crystal in one of Randi's favorite throwback movies. "Baz sure acted like a guy hung up on a woman."

"He's Carl Madison's brother." Shouldn't that say it all?

"You can't hold him accountable for having such

a lousy person as a brother. Our mom is no reflection of who we are."

"He seduced me to get me to cancel the interview."

"Did he say that?"

"Yes!" Well, he hadn't denied it. That was as good as.

"And you didn't knee him in the family jewels?"

"There was enough violence going around."

Kayla nodded, her curly black hair bouncing a little. "That's kind of what I mean, though. I think his feelings changed. He stood up for you, in a white-knight sort of way."

"If you say so."

"Didn't you say that he was going to convince his brother to do a press release absolving you of guilt in the accident?" Kayla asked.

"He was probably lying!"

"He doesn't seem like a man who lies a lot."

"How can you say that? He hid his connection to the Madisons from me."

"But he wasn't lying outright to you. He told you all about having a brother and sister that didn't live in Spain, even a niece and nephew."

"How was I supposed to leap from that to the truth?"

"Well, I don't think he meant you to, but I also think he told you as much truth as he could."

"Only so he could hurt me."

"No, his plan would have helped you more than it would the Madisons."

"You're assuming he was sincere about it."

"I guess I am."

"I'm not."

Her sister didn't keep pushing it. Just gave her a one-armed hug before putting in another romantic comedy.

It was close to midnight a day later when Miranda reached for her phone. She'd ignored several texts and messages from Baz. But she couldn't sleep. The night before had been bad enough, but now she was nearly drunk with exhaustion, only her brain would not shut down. She could not get Baz's deal out of her head, or the prospect of hurting two innocent, defenseless children with her actions.

She dialed his number, almost hoping she woke him from a sound sleep. The only thing better would be for him to be lying awake just like she was. Fat chance of that, though.

The man had no conscience to bother.

He answered on the first ring. "Miranda?"

"Yes, it's me. Didn't your phone tell you who was calling?"

"*Sí*, but I had a hard time believing it. You have not replied to my texts or messages."

"I deleted them without reading or listening to any."

"I see."

"I doubt it." He'd have to have feelings to understand hers.

"But you have called me now."

"That deal you offered me in the car…"

"It was not a deal. I simply outlined what I was willing to do for you."

"In exchange for me not doing the interview. That makes it a deal."

"If I told you I planned to keep my side regardless?"

Her heart stuttered, but she refused to be taken in so easily. "I would not believe you, and if I did, I'd wonder what your angle was."

"All right."

"All right what?"

"I accept you do not trust me at all."

"How could I?" she demanded, her voice low

with pain. "You lied to me from the moment we met."

"I tried very hard *not* to lie to you."

"So you say." That his words were what Kayla said might be true didn't matter. Randi couldn't let it matter. Trusting him would only bring her more pain. "Look, I called because the arguments you made for me not doing the interview are still valid, even if they were made by a lying bastard."

Besides, no matter what she'd threatened, Randi had no desire to go onto national television and humiliate herself by telling the world that she'd got taken in once again by a smooth operator who wanted to use sex as a way to get to her.

"I'm deeply relieved you think so, but not surprised."

"You aren't?" she couldn't stop herself asking.

"No. You are a very compassionate, caring woman, and highly intelligent."

Why did he have to say things like that? "So complimentary to the enemy."

"I do not consider you the enemy."

"Well, I can't say the same about you." Her heart and head might not be in the same place, but he never had to know that.

"I am sorry to hear that."

"So, the deal still stands?"

"I will keep my side of things, yes."

"Okay, I'll need to see the press announcement released and some proof the rest of it is happening before I call the news station and cancel the interview. But don't bother with the apology from Mr. Madison. No way would it be sincere, so really, what's the point?"

"Oh, there is definitely a point." Residual anger laced Baz's voice, and she had to accept that no matter what he'd done to her, Baz was genuinely disgusted by his older brother's behavior.

But that didn't mean he was right. "I don't agree."

"I will make sure everything you want is done. Immediately."

"I want to go back five years and not get behind the wheel, but no one can make that happen," she admitted with more candor than she probably should have.

He made a sound, like her words had hurt him, but that couldn't be right, could it? He'd have to care to hurt on her behalf.

"I wish I could make that happen for you," he said, his voice rich with sincerity she could not trust. "But Jamie is fine now and your life will not implode again. I give you my word."

"For whatever that is worth." She sighed, not wanting to keep sniping. "Hopefully, for both my sake and that of your family, you'll follow through."

"I will." It sounded like a vow.

Randi had a hard time not instinctively trusting that tone. "Okay. I guess we'll see."

He was silent for a few seconds and then he made a sound like he'd made a decision. "There is one stipulation."

No. No way. "Carl Madison doesn't get to insist on anything."

"It is not so onerous, for either of us."

"What are you talking about?"

"I will stay by your side until the day of the interview has passed."

"To make sure I don't go back on my word?" she asked, offended. The fact her heart had leaped at the suggestion wasn't something she wanted to think about. "That's not necessary and you know it."

"*Mi cariña*, admit it—you do not hate my company. And I find yours very enjoyable."

"I'm not your darling."

"Are you so sure about that?"

"You can't want to do this. You have a multibillion-dollar company to run. In Spain!"

"We may both have to make concessions to spend the next days together, but I assure you, I do not find the idea of those weeks in your company onerous in the least."

"Maybe because I didn't spend the last one lying to *you*."

"He wants to do what?"

Miranda pulled the phone away from her ear at Kayla's loud shriek. "You heard me. He wants to spend the next two weeks following me around like a private eye or something."

"Or a puppy dog." Kayla's laughter came across the line.

"Yeah, no. Basilio Perez is no lost puppy."

"You can say that after the way he followed you on the MAX?" Kayla kept teasing.

"So he's a control freak and I wasn't doing what he wanted."

"Or you know, he was having an Andreas in New York moment."

Kayla had told Randi about how she and Andreas got together, but this was not like that and she told her sister so.

"So, are you going along with it?"

"I want the stuff he promised. I want my life back. I think his plan has a better chance than the interview of defusing the situation long-term."

"As much as I want the world to know the truth about you, because you're my sister and I think everyone should think you're as great as I do, I agree. Darn it."

Randi smiled. "You're a good sister, but I think this is the right thing to do."

And that was why she found herself packing a bag to join Baz at his executive condo that day after work. He'd offered to stay in her apartment, but she didn't want any more memories she had to forget haunting her in her own home.

Besides, his condo had two bedrooms. Her apartment only had one.

CHAPTER NINE

RANDI LIFTED HER hand to knock on the door of Baz's penthouse, but somehow she couldn't make the final connection between her knuckle and the wood.

Was she really going to do this?

Could she spend two weeks in the company of a man who had used sex to convince her to do what he wanted? More important, a man who had managed to break down the protective walls she'd built around her heart only to decimate it.

Her internal debate was interrupted by the door swinging open.

Baz stood there, his expression hard to read. "You made it."

"Yes."

He stepped back and waved her inside, grabbing her bag as she went by. "I'll just put this in the bedroom."

"You'd better mean *my* bedroom."

He inclined his head in acknowledgment as he walked away.

Rather than follow him down the hall to the bedrooms, she went into the main living area, but stopped short at what she found there. The table had been set with linens, crystal and candlesticks. Soft jazz played over the condo's built-in sound system, a fire was lit in the gas fireplace and the lights set to a soft glow.

Baz came up beside her. "Are you hungry? The food is from that steak house you told me about."

Her mouth watered, but she gazed at him stonily. "It looks awfully romantic for a dinner between two adversaries."

"We are not adversaries."

"Just because you say something doesn't make it true."

He didn't reply, but took her arm gently and led her to the table. Once he'd helped her into her seat, Baz lit the candles.

"That's really not necessary."

"I think it is."

"We aren't on a date." She shook out her napkin with brisk movements before sliding it over her lap. "I'm here because I have to be."

"I am aware, *mi hermosa*."

"Stop with the Spanish endearments."

"You prefer English ones?"

"That's not what I meant and you know it."

"I know that our steaks will be cold before we eat them at this rate."

The meat was delicious, as were the garlic mashed potatoes and lightly sauced sautéed vegetables that came with it. The good food, soft music and warm ambience helped Randi to relax, when she thought there was no way she could ever be at peace in Baz's company again.

Baz kept the conversation light and away from topics that might blow up between them, which wasn't to say he didn't talk about anything personal. He seemed intent on her getting to know him and his history. The Spaniard regaled her with stories of his various stepmothers and their attempts to tame or bring out the refined in Armand Perez by turns.

"*Madre*, she always wanted *Papá* to play the big businessman about town, but her successor was more interested in starting yet another family. *Papá*, not so much."

Randi made a noncommittal sound.

Baz showed no frustration with her lack of response, just as he had chosen to ignore her desultory forays into conversation throughout the meal. "No, Armand Perez had three children, and that was enough for him. But she would not give up, hosting dinners *en famille*, dropping baby name books around the house, redecorating the nursery."

"*En famille* is French, not Spanish."

"I may not have gone to university, but I am not ignorant." He flashed her his all-too-sexy smile. "I am fluent in five languages. French is one of them."

"Ignorance isn't always about formal education."

"So I believe."

"For instance, having a bevy of degrees wouldn't have stopped you from being anything but ignorant when it comes to the feelings of others." Needing to get away from him, she stood up and carried her dishes into the kitchen.

The man had used her own body's response against her, and if he'd realized it, her *heart*. But he thought that somehow the whys of them going to bed together the first time didn't matter. Because why? Because the sex was great? Great sex wasn't going to stop her heart from being broken.

They'd had it. More than once and her heart was a shattered organ in her chest.

"You can leave them. A maid comes in the morning and again in the afternoon."

"Then she can deal with what is in the sink. I'm not leaving a dirty table overnight."

"Naturally not." He placed his dishes and cutlery with hers. "I wasn't trying to ignore your feelings, Miranda."

"I don't know how you can say that." All the relaxation that dinner had managed drained out of her, leaving Randi's body tense and her heart beating just a little fast. She stepped away from the sink, and Baz, before she turned to look up at him.

"Five years ago, when everything happened, I was only nineteen. Despite my past, I was still a very naive nineteen-year-old. I believed the best of people. When Davy came along, I thought he was really interested in me. My heart was bruised from my almost fiancé's desertion and I soaked up his attention like a sponge. Do you want to know what I discovered on the one and only night we had sex?"

"What? What did you find out?" Baz asked, his voice husky, his accent just that little bit thicker.

"That he was only dating me, that *he'd had sex with me*, to get the dirt on the girl who had hit Carl and Tiffany Madison's son with her car."

"That bastard. What is this Davy's last name?"

"Seriously? If he's a bastard, what are you?"

Baz winced, but he caught her gaze with his deep brown one, sending some kind of message she could not interpret. "I wasn't looking for dirt."

"No, you were just looking for malleability. I don't know how you can claim to have had no intention of hurting me. You'd have to be an emotionless monster not to know that doing the same thing to me as Davy, the enterprising reporter, would more than hurt. It would devastate."

"I didn't know about him."

"But you did know that you engineered our meeting with the express purpose of convincing me not to do the interview. Then you..." Randi had to take several deep breaths before she could collect her thoughts and emotions. "You decided to use sex as a weapon against me just like he did."

"Not like him. I wasn't trying to get a juicy story."

"No, just manipulate me with my body's reaction to you." With her heart, not that she believed he would understand how deep it had gone for her so quickly.

She wasn't even sure Baz believed in romantic

love. The way he talked about his father's marriages indicated a real cynicism toward the concept.

"I did plan to use sex to get you to trust me," he admitted, like it pained him to do so. "I needed you to listen with an open mind when I told you why doing the interview would be a mistake."

"Don't pretend you had a single concern about me and how the interview would impact me when you settled on your plan to seduce me."

He frowned, his dark brows drawing together. "But how it would impact you matters to me *now*, very much."

"And I'm supposed to believe you?"

"I would like it very much if you did."

"I don't know if I can." She wasn't being stubborn. Her heart hurt, every second of every day since she'd discovered his deceit. "When I realized who and what Davy was, I was humiliated. And hurt. But nothing in even the same universe to what I felt the moment I realized you were Carl Madison's brother, that everything between us had been part of an agenda."

"I cannot change why we met, but I will prove to you that we are too good together to walk away from each other over it. That your feelings do indeed matter to me."

"I don't know how."

"Leave that to me. I am an excellent problem-solver."

"I'm a problem you have to solve?"

"The situation between us is the problem. You are the most passionate, engaging, beautiful woman I have ever met."

"Now I know you are lying. I am no super-model."

"Good. I would not be nearly as attracted to you if you were, no matter how charming your personality."

Oh, goodness. She was going to fall right back into this man's bed if she didn't watch herself. "Do you have any romantic comedies for that expensive media system in the living room?"

"That *expensive* media system has access to several movie-streaming services. I am sure you can find whatever movie you would prefer."

"Okay, then."

"*Bien*, I am glad to please."

He surprised her by sitting with her to watch *French Kiss*.

"I can't believe you've never seen this one. It's a classic."

"I admit I watch movies rarely and never romantic ones."

"I love them. I want to believe in happy beginnings."

"I thought the term was happy ending?"

"An ending implies that's all there is, but the couple getting together is only the beginning of the adventure."

"Perhaps if my father understood that, he would not have married so many times."

"Some people think relationships shouldn't take any work."

"You do not agree?"

"Of course not. Every relationship requires effort, whether it's with a friend, a sister, a parent, a coworker. Why would maintaining emotional connection with your partner be any different?"

Basilio cut his connection to the conference call. He needed to get back to Spain. The big question was, could he convince Miranda to accompany him?

For a woman whose only committed relationship had crashed and burned five years earlier, she had insights that put his father's attitudes to shame. Basilio respected and loved his father, but Miranda's words had resonated with him. He knew that when things got tough or even mildly challenging in his marriages, his father started looking elsewhere.

The idea that the wedding was just the beginning of the journey, not the end, was the antithesis of how Basilio had grown up. But he liked it.

If he was to marry, it would be to a woman who felt as Miranda did.

For that to even be a possibility, he had to convince her that he would not hurt her again.

And to do that, he needed to take her to Spain, to introduce her to his world and show her that she fit in it.

"I can't leave right now. You know we're in the middle of opening a second Kayla's for Kids facility." Randi had returned to Baz's condo again that evening to a similar setting to the night before.

The table was once again set beautifully, this time a gorgeous oversize bouquet of richly colored fall blooms in the center of the table.

Who had he asked to discover that while Randi

did not have a favorite flower, she preferred those of the season?

"My executive assistant has found someone eminently qualified to fill in for you."

"What? You can't just bring in a temp to do something like this."

"She is not a temp. She is, in fact, a woman with a great deal of experience with facilities of this kind. She will work on not only bringing in new funding, but also getting the second facility up and running."

"You're trying to make me obsolete with my sister's charity?"

"No." He looked genuinely offended. "What kind of man do you think I am? No, do not answer that, *cariña*. I want you with me in Spain."

"You make it sound like we're in a relationship and you're trying to keep me with you."

"Doesn't it?"

"We are not in a relationship." They weren't. Whatever they had ended when she found out he was just using her.

The memory of him saying they could make a baby when she told him she wasn't pregnant assailed her. With another guy, that would have been a throwaway comment. Or sarcasm at the very least.

Not Basilio Perez, though.

But then what did she know about him? She'd thought he was a random billionaire she'd run into on the sidewalk, that there was no way he could have an agenda. That he was a safe lover, if temporary.

None of that had turned out to be true.

"Will you come to Spain?"

"Do I really have a choice?"

"We always have a choice."

"This whole staying together for the next two weeks is ridiculous."

"But you agreed to it."

"I'm not going anywhere unless Kayla agrees to this replacement you found for me. And I'm not going to spend my time there on vacation. You'll need to make sure I can stay available via phone, video calls and my email."

"Despite what you clearly think of me, I am not a man of the Dark Ages. We have all the modern technologies in our home."

"We? Our?"

"My father lives in my hacienda when he is in Madrid."

"Is he there now?" she asked suspiciously.

"No, in fact. He is visiting his latest fiancée's family in Monaco."

"She's not Spanish?"

"Why should this surprise you? Certainly you've worked out by now that Carlos and Gracia's mother is American."

"And your mother?"

"From Catalonia."

"That makes sense. You are *very* Spanish."

"What does that mean?"

"No one would mistake you for an Englishman, despite that being the accent you speak with using this language."

"I would imagine not."

She shook her head. She wasn't even sure what *she* meant. It was just a feeling, but it wasn't like she had a lot of experience with the nuances between European cultures.

Surprisingly, Kayla had no trouble with Randi taking off for Spain in the middle of the new facility setup. "This woman Baz's executive assistant found for us has experience neither one of us has. She'll be a great resource."

Randi couldn't deny it. The new shelter liaison

had started her job running, preempting several potential problems in the first few hours she'd been there.

"She would be a better manager for the shelters," Randi admitted.

"No, but she will be a great resource and she's making it possible for you to visit Spain."

"It's not a vacation. Baz is forcing me to go so he can ensure I don't do the interview after promising not to."

"Are you sure about that?"

"What else?"

"The man fell for you and he's looking for the time and opportunity to prove to you that he's not the monster you've decided he is."

"Kayla," Randi groaned. "I know you found happiness with your longtime best friend, but not every guy is as trustworthy as Andreas."

Randi wasn't sure *any* man was. Her trust factor was at zero right now.

"Andreas is not exactly perfect."

"Don't be telling falsehood to your sister." Andreas's voice came over the phone from somewhere near Kayla.

Kayla and Randi both laughed.

"Well, he's not lacking self-confidence anyway,"

Randi said with a smile, surprised at the feeling of lightness in her chest.

"Trust me, he's hurt me. More than once. Loving someone means you figure out how to forgive the stuff that can't be changed."

"And if you can't?"

"Then that relationship isn't good for you."

"You make it sound so simple."

"Life is anything but."

"You know I've always wanted to travel to Europe."

"And you know that Andreas and I would have happily taken you. This isn't about seeing the bullfighters of Madrid."

Randi shivered. "No, it's not about that, for sure."

"You want to find out if you can learn to trust the man again."

"Isn't that just opening myself up for more pain?"

"Life isn't just complicated, it's risky, but if you don't take the risks, you can't have the rewards."

Randi didn't reply. Her thoughts were too jumbled.

"Randi?" Andreas asked.

"I'm here. Kayla gave you her phone."

"I may have confiscated it."

"What's going on?"

"It is just that I see a lot of similarity between myself and Baz."

"You do?"

"I had him investigated."

"You knew he was related to Carl Madison?"

"I found out the same day you did. The final report came in about an hour before your phone call to Kayla. I hadn't even told my wife yet."

"You were looking out for me."

"Always. You are *my* sister now, too."

"Thank you."

"No thanks necessary. Just give the man a chance. He's ruthless in business, but he is not underhanded. He has integrity."

"He deceived me."

"He did, but do you really think he only took you to bed to get your agreement to cancel the interview?"

"He admitted it."

"He may have been deceiving himself."

"Or not."

"Or not. But if your sister hadn't known me better than I knew myself, if she hadn't stuck by my side that first time I ended our romantic relationship, remained my friend, I would have been lost. I would not be the man I am today."

"Kayla is pretty special."

"So are you, Miranda Smith."

Just not special enough for Baz to want her for herself and not what she could do for him.

Basilio bit back a sigh as Miranda accepted a fizzy mineral water from the flight attendant, her usual warmth and enthusiasm glaringly absent. She wasn't rude. She did not pout. But the bright inner light he'd grown enamored of was not shining from her.

There was no pleasure in knowing that his deception was the most likely culprit.

He did not understand how his actions could have such a profound effect on her after such a short time together, but then his own reaction to Miranda confused Basilio. The day she'd found out Basilio's connection to Carlos's family, her pain, her clear sense of betrayal, both had made Basilio feel like a monster. He'd been unable to allow her to just walk away, and the interview had been the last thing on his mind when he chased after her.

He had made efforts to prevent her from ejecting him completely from her life that he would not have made for any other woman.

Again, his desire to bring her to Spain had nothing to do with protecting his family and everything to do with protecting something precious.

It smacked loudly of an emotional decision. Basilio did not do overly emotional. It was too dangerous a barometer for rational choices.

And yet here he was, on the Perez jet, sitting in his favorite leather chair facing the table he usually used to work, Miranda right beside him, her inner fire banked.

He could not leave it like that.

He needed a conversational gambit, something to spark the natural curiosity she'd shown so far. Even after she'd become angry with him, she hadn't been able to hide her interest in his life back in Spain. That was why he'd taken the risk of trying to convince her to come with him to his home in Madrid. "You will like the hacienda."

She looked up from her e-reader, a tiny spark of interest flaring before she blanked her face. "Will I?"

"It is over two hundred years old."

"Inside Madrid?"

"On the outskirts of the city, but there are many historic buildings in the city center."

Triumph rang through him when curiosity flared in her pretty gray eyes. "When I lived in Southern California, one of my favorite things to do was visiting Old Town San Diego. The buildings were so beautiful, the museums that showed an old way of life, fascinating."

"The Mission Style architecture there has a great deal of Spanish influence."

"Yes, it does."

"Hopefully you will find the original to the inspiration as interesting."

She set her e-reader down on the table. "You really want me to see this trip as some kind of vacation, don't you?"

"I would prefer you were looking forward to the benefits, yes." He wanted to show her his home, had a completely irrational desire for her to fall in love with it.

She gave him a skeptical look, her posture stiff. "As opposed to the detriments?"

"And what are those, do you think?"

"I don't know," she said with heavy sarcasm. "What about having to leave the job I love, the shelter's clients that are so important to me, at the last minute?"

"But you've left them in good hands and you will stay connected, *sí*?"

"That is the hope. Regardless, I wasn't planning on an international trip right now. Or any trip of any kind, and I know you know that." She adjusted her fitted suit jacket, so unlike her usual clothing, but no less alluring.

The blue-gray fabric brought out the color of her eyes, the cut highlighting her elegant curves. Basilio wanted nothing more than to peel away the layers, revealing the entrancing body beneath.

"Life is full of surprises." Like meeting a woman who played such havoc with his self-restraint.

"Not all of them are pleasant."

"But surely a trip to Spain is."

"Just because you love your home doesn't mean everyone will."

"But you are not just everyone."

She frowned at him, her gaze filled with wariness. "Whatever that means."

"I find it better to accept and seek to gain from life's little vagaries, rather than get mired in the plan that might have been."

"You? Mr. Control Freak?"

He would have denied the moniker, but thought now was not the time. "Indeed."

"I have a hard time seeing it."

"You think I was anticipating a trip to America a week ago?" He'd had to cancel important meetings and work at inconvenient hours to stay as long as he had.

"I suppose not." She chewed on her bottom lip, thinking. "I didn't make you come, though, did I?"

"No, but meeting you was the benefit of doing so." She looked like she was going to protest that, so he continued. "Business rarely goes exactly as one might expect. I've purchased properties I didn't expect to, let go of ones I thought I would initially keep. And all those things have worked out for the best."

She sighed, her eyes warm with unexpected compassion. "I suppose all those new stepmoms taught you to roll with the punches early on."

"Perhaps you are right." Really, there was no maybe about it.

Basilio had figured out early on that he could rail against the constant changes his father's love life imposed on him, or he could seek to thrive in each new circumstance. Basilio chose to thrive.

"I think my experiences did the opposite for

me." She looked away to the window in silence for long seconds before turning her head to meet his gaze again. Hers filled with unexpected vulnerability. "I don't like surprises. They make me nervous. Change is always hard for me."

"I imagine with a mother as unstable as yours, you learned your own lessons early. Like not all surprises are good ones."

Her hands fisted in her lap, her gray eyes widening in surprise. "You know about my mom?"

He nodded. "I wanted to wait for you to tell me, but you have probably already figured out that patience is not one of my virtues."

"Considering how fast you got me into bed, I'd say not."

And he wanted her there again. "You did not complain."

"No, but then I was convinced you couldn't have any agenda but wanting sex. Even if you weren't offering anything more than a night of pleasure, that felt safe to me."

"Despite your lack of experience, you accepted the lack of commitment with equanimity." Not to mention their instant focus on the physical. "It surprised me." And delighted him by turn.

"Believing there could be no way you were lying

about your motives for getting me into bed gave me a false sense of security. I wasn't looking for a long-term relationship. I was looking for honesty."

"Considering your past, I can now understand why that would have been so important to you." He hated that Miranda no longer trusted him, or felt safe being physically intimate with him.

He'd been unable to convince her that he no longer had ulterior motives where she was concerned, and he knew that was his own fault.

She fidgeted with the buttons on her jacket, picked up her e-reader and then put it back down again. Finally, she took a deep breath, let it out and asked, "So, you had me investigated?"

"I had done that early on." Surely she would have realized that by now? "I ordered a deeper look. I got the report last night."

"I wondered what you were reading while I watched my movies. I thought it was work."

"It was, for part of the night. Being away from my office has been a challenge."

"Was looking at a Portland property a lie, too?" she asked, her eyes narrowed.

Her irritation should not have been a turn-on, but he found her feistiness exciting. Doing his best to ignore his body's response to her, he answered,

"No. There is an old hotel I was interested in, but ultimately it would require millions in remodeling to bring it up to present codes and update the facility to the standards of other similar Perez Holdings. It's a beautiful property, though."

"That's too bad."

He hoped that was disappointment he heard in her voice, and that a little of it at least was because without a property he'd have little reason—that she would accept at present anyway—to return to Portland.

Deciding to test that theory, he offered, "My broker found me another potential property."

Her gaze locked onto his. "He did?"

"Yes."

"What did you think of it?" she asked with poorly disguised eagerness.

Relief that she still wanted a reason for him to return to Portland, even if she didn't want to admit it, made him speak with warm enthusiasm. "It has a lot of potential."

"So you'll come back to Portland."

"Sí." He smiled. "For more than the hotel." And what she did with that knowledge was up to her.

CHAPTER TEN

THE WARINESS CAME back into Randi's expression before she turned her head to look out the window again. "Anyway, you know about my mom."

Surprised by the return to a subject he could tell was difficult for her, he answered honestly. "I know what the investigator was able to find out in a twenty-four-hour window. She lost custody of you to your father, with no option for visitation, when you were six. Your parents divorced and your mother spent a couple of years in a psychiatric facility."

"Pretending to be crazy." Miranda looked back at him, her gray eyes haunted. "So she wouldn't go to jail for trying to drown me in my bath."

All the air left Basilio's lungs. Miranda's mother had tried to kill her? No. His mind could not accept that; he could not accept the risk that she might have died before they'd ever met. "Pretending?" Didn't the woman have to be insane to have tried to kill her daughter? Wasn't that the very definition of an imbalance?

"She was high on her drug of choice at the time and furious with my father for refusing to give her money to buy more. So she decided to take away something he loved more than her. At least that's how she saw it."

"By trying to drown you?"

"My dad caught her."

"*Gracias a Dios!* What if he had not been there?"

Miranda's vulnerable gaze said she'd considered that possibility, many times, maybe even had nightmares about it. "He kept a close eye on me with her, but he couldn't always be there. He was that time, though, and it saved my life."

"And instead of going to prison, she went into a mental facility?"

"You get it." There was a lessening of the haunting in Miranda's stormy gray eyes. "You really do. So many people, they kept telling me I needed to forgive her, have a relationship with her, but she just hurts people. She uses them. Only my dad and then Kayla got that, but she'd hurt them, too."

Something about his acceptance gave Miranda

peace, and Basilio could feel nothing but gratitude for that. She deserved a lessening of her burden, and if he could give it to her, he would. "Not everyone who looks sympathetic on paper really is."

"Exactly." Miranda managed a small smile. "She's always been good at playing the crazy card when she's caught out. But since she has always refused any kind of therapy or medical treatment outside of her time in the hospital, I've never really bought into the sincerity of it. I've worked with many people truly challenged by mental illness in my job. Some who wanted to learn ways to better cope, some who didn't, but none who could turn it on and off like a tap the way my mother has always done."

"She tormented your life, didn't she?"

"Very much until I was six, more than my dad realized. Not so much after, but because of my grandparents, she's remained in the periphery of my life."

"They believe she's not responsible for her actions," he guessed.

Miranda's grimace told him he'd guessed right. "They're wonderful people who always see the best in anyone."

"I do not like thinking of that woman having access to you, even a step removed." He wanted to pull Miranda into his arms.

She wrapped her arms around herself, making him want to comfort her even more. "Honestly? I don't, either. I've managed to avoid seeing her since I was fifteen, and that only happened because Grandma got the time of a visit wrong and my mother was still at her house when Dad and I showed up."

His mouth twisted with cynicism. "Some mistake."

She laughed, the sound dry and harsh, but humor all the same. "Right? My dad arranged all future visits at our house so it couldn't happen again. I think I'll always fear her because she has no conscience. If she thinks hurting me, or them, or anyone else, will get her what she wants in the moment, she'll do it. No compunction, no regret."

"I am very sorry." A plethora of stepmothers seemed like a very normal childhood in comparison. "Is that why you don't like boats?"

"I know it doesn't make any sense, but yes. I mean, seas and rivers aren't the same at all. Only in my head, water is water."

Basilio flipped up the two armrests between their seats and then put his arm around her, laying his other hand over hers fisted together in her lap. "Your head is the only one that counts in this matter."

"Talking about her with you, I realize I've made her into a bogeyman, but I don't need to."

"You love your grandparents, so you worry for them."

She nodded. "Family, yeah? But still, you've helped me let go of a sense of doom that has been shadowing my life for too long, even after I moved away from everyone in my family. I have to thank you for that."

"No thanks necessary." She deserved full-on happiness.

She looked away for a second, but then met his gaze again, hers open in a way he wasn't sure he'd ever see again. "Until I met you, I hadn't had a bath to relax or for the sake of enjoyment in almost two decades," she admitted as her body melted into his.

"If I had known—"

"No, that was a good thing, the way I felt safe in water with you." She sat up, pulling away from him, gently pushing his hand away, too. "What-ever came after, you helped me to overcome a lifelong fear."

"But you are still uncertain about boats." And him.

"I think so." But she sounded more speculative than certain.

It made him wonder if he could help her feel safe in his presence and overcome a phobia at the same time. "Perhaps I can help you change that."

The look she gave him was blatantly consid-ering, but tinged with hope he wasn't sure she wanted him to see. "Maybe."

"You're very noncommittal."

"Wary."

"Ouch."

"Are you surprised?"

"No, but I wish it was not that way."

"Why? Why do you care?"

"Do I have to have a reason? Is it not enough that I do? Very much." Her honesty deserved his own. No matter how uncomfortable the admis-sion made him.

"Thank you."

"For?" Caring? He could not stop himself.

"Being honest."

* * *

A strange expression came over Baz's face. "When I told you about spending the next two weeks together..." He paused, looking uncharacteristically uncertain.

"Yes? What about it?"

"You assumed it was a requirement Carlos had insisted on."

"To make sure I didn't go back on my word." Like she was the one people had to worry about lying.

"There was never any doubt that you would keep your word."

"Thanks for that, but it's a bit late, don't you think?"

"It was never a consideration." His tone brooked no argument.

But that didn't make any sense. "Then why say I had to be chaperoned like a recalcitrant teenager on a bad date?"

Basilio loosened his tie, his movement jerky. "It was not a requirement at all." He made the fantastic admission and then waited for her reaction, his expression stoic, only a slight tic in his jaw giving away that just maybe he was a little nervous.

"What? That makes no sense." On the verge of

yelling like a harpy, Randi made a concerted effort to modulate her tone. "I'm here on this ridiculously luxurious plane with you, flying to Spain, during a crucial time for Kayla's for Kids because I didn't have a choice."

He winced. "I hope that is not true."

"Of course it is." But was it?

Had she really agreed to this crazy trip because she felt cornered? Her conscience pricked because she knew that deep inside, where she hid feelings that she knew could hurt her, Randi had to acknowledge the truth.

She was on her way to Spain because the thought of never seeing Baz again had been ten times more terrible than the idea of spending time in his company, whatever the reason.

"I never lied to you," he said quickly.

"You let me believe I didn't have a choice."

"Say rather, I did not work very hard at dissuading you."

Had he tried at all? Her muddled brain couldn't be sure in that moment what was real and what was not. "Why? Why mislead me again?"

"I have told you, I believe we have something special, something worth figuring out a way back to."

He couldn't be implying what it sounded like,

but she had to be sure. "Are you saying you love me?" she asked, hearing the disbelief in her own voice.

"Romantic love is something I always promised myself I would never fall prey to." The words sounded sure, but his tone? It sounded hollow.

"Because of how easily your dad falls in and out of love."

Baz inclined his head in agreement. "His has been a life lesson on the subject, certainly."

Her heart died a little at hearing those words, but love was not the main issue here. Was it? "You deceived me. Again."

"If you consider it, you will realize I was very careful *not* to lie to you."

She tried very hard to remember the conversations they'd had about the trip verbatim. "You never actually agreed with me when I assumed it was a requirement of Carl Madison's, or when I said I had no choice about coming to Spain."

"No, I did not."

"But you still let *me* believe it."

"When I disagreed, you disregarded my words."

Randi should have been more angry, but she wasn't. This time felt different. Was it because she had ignored him when he said he wasn't her enemy? Maybe it was opening up to Basilio and having him take her part immediately. Maybe it was the fact that he had managed to convince his brother to do exactly as Basilio had promised he would. Maybe it was even the fact that he'd risked her ire to make a way for them to reconnect.

Or maybe it was just the fact that while they'd been having casual sex and friendship on the side, her heart had gotten involved.

Whatever the reason, Randi wanted Baz to make this right, to convince her she hadn't been duped again.

"Baz…" She let her voice trail off, not sure what she wanted to say.

He took her hand again, holding it tightly in his own. "You told me very firmly you would not believe the truth."

"What truth?"

"That regardless of whether you canceled the interview, I would make sure Carlos followed through on the things I had promised."

She hadn't canceled the interview until after she'd seen proof of that, but Basilio had even gotten his own PR people involved in planning and executing the best strategy for clearing Randi's name without her having to bare her soul in front of millions of strangers. They'd video-conferenced after she'd agreed to make the trip to Spain, the very savvy PR reps asking questions that helped shape a brilliant campaign to protect her. The head of the team had mentioned that Baz had called them in the very night she'd discovered his connection to the Madisons, before Randi had agreed to give up the interview.

She wasn't sure what to do with that information.

Unwilling to pull away from his touch again, and even more unwilling to examine why, she licked her lips nervously then admitted, "Andreas and Kayla appreciated his letters of apology more than I did."

"You did not believe in Carlos's sincerity."

"No, I didn't."

"He is sincere, though, if not for the reason I wish it were so." And Baz's espresso gaze said he was, too. Sincere, that was.

"Oh, really?"

"His actions have caused me to curtail my support of his company and threaten to cut it off all together." Baz's implacable tone said he wasn't kidding or exaggerating.

"But he's your family."

"And he acted abysmally. Would you stand up for your mother in similar circumstances?"

"I wouldn't stand up for her at all, under *any* circumstances." Randi laid her free hand on Basilio's thigh. "But your brother has not given you reason to withdraw your support. He hasn't hurt you or turned on you."

At least to Randi's knowledge. Baz was the one who had punched his brother in the face. For insulting Randi.

She didn't know what she could or should believe right then.

"His actions against you, a compassionate, caring, *honest* woman, were enough to precipitate my own."

Was he speaking the truth? And if he was, what did that mean for them?

She couldn't trust him, her mind insisted. Only her heart wanted to believe. "And now Carl Madison is genuinely sorry because his actions had consequences he wasn't expecting."

"*Sí.*"

"That is more believable than he had a sudden change of heart."

"One can only hope he will eventually see the error of his ways, but if he does not…" Baz paused, his expression taking on a ruthlessness she'd never actually seen directed toward herself. "He is aware the order of protection you took out against him is the least of his worries if he comes anywhere near you or attempts to contact you in any way."

"Wow." Randi hadn't been expecting that. "Okay."

"I have arranged for regular visits from his children. I believe they need the influence of their Spanish family."

"That's pretty arrogant, but I can't disagree. If for nothing else, his children deserve to be raised with a taste of their heritage. Just because he decided to reject it doesn't mean they're going to want to." And after her experience with Kayla, Randi was particularly sensitive about the idea of withholding children from loving, decent grandparents.

Her sister's childhood would have been so different if she'd had the support of their grandparents, like Randi had.

"I agree." The words showed Baz was listening to her, but his focus was fixed on her lips. Again.

There was no doubt the man wanted her. Her desire for him was simmering under the surface, hard to control, even harder to hide.

Heat suffused Randi's body and she couldn't do a thing about it. He wanted to kiss her and she wanted that kiss. So much.

The muscles of his thigh bunched under her hand and she realized only then how dangerous that connection was. She yanked her hand away.

"Don't." He reached for her wrist.

"Don't what?"

He placed her hand back on his thigh, pressing it down with his. "I like when you touch me."

"But—"

He placed his finger against her open mouth, but instead of pressing to quiet her, he traced first her upper lip and then her lower one. "Such a pretty mouth."

Desire shivered through her, her vaginal walls spasming with need. Oh, man. She was in trouble if such a small caress had this effect on her.

He leaned down and she didn't do a single thing to stop him, didn't tell him no, just sat there waiting for what she knew was coming. Her brain warned her she was on a slippery, dangerous path, but her body was not listening.

Neither was her heart.

The kiss, when it came, was soft, a caress of lips against lips, no tongue, no urgency. And it went all the way to her soul. One hand remained over hers; the other came up to cup her nape, under her hair, and hers came up of its own volition to rest against his chest.

The tender, almost chaste kiss went on for long moments, bridging a gap she didn't know something so simple could do.

It was terrifying how much the press of his mouth against hers impacted her.

It was that fear that made her break the kiss and pull away from him. "You shouldn't have done that."

"I disagree. Kissing you is never a mistake."

"I'm sure your family would not agree."

"Meet my father before you decide to speak for him. He will adore you."

"I thought you said he wasn't going to be in Madrid when we arrived."

"He will not, but you will meet him."

"You're talking like we have a future together."

"It does sound like that, doesn't it?"

"How am I supposed to take that? You don't even believe in love."

"Erotic love, no, but I love my family. Even my disreputable brother, who has much to do to earn my respect again, if that can be done."

She shook her head, trying to clear it. The man was too persuasive and confusing. "No more kissing."

"I cannot promise that. You are very kissable."

"You're being ridiculous."

"The truth is foolish to you?"

"No. That's not what I… Listen, you can't just go around kissing me. We aren't dating anymore."

"I would like to fix that."

"You deceived me a second time. How could I *ever* trust you again?"

"Perhaps you could examine my intentions in both cases?"

"I'd rather know you were never going to lie to me again, by omission or commission," she clarified when he opened his mouth to deny actually lying again.

"This is important to you?"

"Would you like knowing I was happy to deceive you?"

"No."

"Then?"

He was silent for almost a full minute, considering. "I can make that promise."

"Now I just have to believe it." But the fact he'd

really thought about it went a long way toward her doing so.

A brief flare of pain flashed over his handsome features. "That is the hope, *cariña*."

"You're not going to stop using endearments on me, are you?"

"Does it truly offend you?"

"No, it's just…" Too pleasant. Too seductive. Too intimate. But to admit any of that would be to admit she still had feelings for him when he didn't even believe in those feelings. "It irritates me."

"Are we not both committed to honesty between us?"

She sighed. "Yes."

"So?"

"It did irritate me." Right after she found out about his reason for engineering their meeting, but now the endearments were part of that slippery slope that both enamored and scared her.

"Now?" he pressed.

"I like it too much," she admitted, not entirely sure this full honesty between them was a good thing.

"That is good to hear."

"You are a very annoying man."

"And you are the one woman I want."

"Right now."

"Do you want promises for the future?"

"No, of course not. I don't want anything from you."

"Are you lying to me again, or only to yourself now?"

"I'm tired. I think I'll get some shut-eye." Not waiting for him to respond, she reclined her seat and closed her eyes, trying to shut him out.

But nothing could make her any less aware of the gorgeous, tantalizingly sexual man sitting beside her on the private jet.

No wonder Baz didn't mind having his father living with him.

His home was a darn palace. A very private palace. Hidden away at the end of a long drive with access via a wrought iron gate that slid back when Baz had pressed something on his phone, the exterior stucco of the giant three-story abode was painted a traditional pastel with white trim. The enormous house was surrounded completely by a second-story balcony, with decorative railing. It served as shade for the oversize slate porch on the ground floor that also wrapped around the stately building.

The grounds looked like something out of a *How*

to Garden for Rich People book, laid out in perfect geometric patterns, each bush trimmed into submission, every blade of grass cut just so and a pristine green. Deep-red carnations filled the flower beds on either side of the double-size, eight-foot-high front doors.

Baz pulled his sleek Jaguar to a stop on the circular drive laid with white pebble just as a butler in a smart black suit opened the door on the left. Seriously? He had a butler? With a home this size, he probably had a whole army of servants.

Randi stared out the window, making no move to open her car door. She craned her head, trying to see as much as she could without actually getting out. "Good grief!"

"What?" Baz asked, his own door already open and his seat belt off.

Randi just shook her head, startling when the door beside her opened without her touching it.

The butler stepped back from the car. "Welcome to Casa Clavel, Miss Smith."

Feeling like she'd stepped into some kind of fantasy, Randi made herself climb out of the luxury sports car. "Um…*gracias*. I'm happy to be here," she lied in Spanish.

What she was, was overwhelmed.

The butler nodded and then turned to Baz, who

had gotten out and come around the car. "Welcome home, sir," he said in Spanish.

"It is very good to be home, Emilio." Baz replied in the same language, his body relaxed in a way she hadn't seen since meeting him.

"You call this place home?" she asked with disbelief.

"What else would you have me call the place where I live?" Humor laced his voice as he offered her his hand.

Feeling out of place and in need of a connection to reality, she took it. "Royalty would be comfortable living here."

"And have stayed behind its walls throughout the years. It was built in the mid-eighteenth century."

"Though it has remained in the same family for more than two centuries, Casa Clavel has been completely remodeled and refurbished as recently as five years ago," the butler offered with obvious pride.

"I wouldn't expect anything less."

Neither man seemed to detect the sarcasm lacing her words.

The inside was every bit as imposing as the outside, and yet somehow felt like a home. Like a place she could stay without feeling like she didn't belong. Which was totally weird, considering the fact that no way could Randi *belong* in a place like this.

She didn't even try to hide her gawking as she took in the soaring ceilings, giant foyer and grand staircase. The floors were marble, a huge gold drape pulled back between the foyer and what looked to be a living room the size of a gymnasium, but way more elegant with its cream, black and gold accented decor.

Baz squeezed her hand, giving her a reassuring smile. "There is a conservatory in the back of the house, where we have citrus trees that bear fruit year-round, and we grow more of the carnations the house is named for. It is my favorite place to have breakfast and to relax."

"Of course it has a conservatory." She looked around at the massive rooms, halls leading to more living space and the giant chandelier hanging in the center of the foyer. "My entire apartment complex would fit in this place."

"It is only about eighteen thousand square feet."

"Only?" she asked faintly as another man, not the butler, walked by, carrying her luggage.

"Most modern-built mansions of this caliber are twice as large."

"That's insane. Who needs that much room?"

Okay, maybe billionaires did, for entertaining or something.

Baz shrugged. "I would say I do. The staff inhabits the top floor. They have their own recreation room, in addition to sitting rooms in each of their suites."

And the rest of this massive hacienda was for Baz and his family. It *was* an apartment complex. "How many bedrooms in a place like this?"

"There are quarters for eight live-in staff members, though not all are occupied, six suites in the family hall and ten guest rooms on the other side of the house."

Ginormous could be good. Her room would be on the other side of the house from his. Distance would make it easier for Randi to stay away from temptation.

"Would you like to refresh yourself from the journey?" the butler asked.

"Yes, sure. That would be great." If she didn't get away from Baz soon, it was going to be her doing the kissing.

And that way lay nothing but pain.

"I'll take her up," Baz told the black-clad man.

"Very good, sir."

"Would you like a tray brought up?" an older

woman, who Randi assumed was the housekeeper, asked.

"*Sí.* Something light," Baz replied before Randi could tell the woman not to go to any trouble.

Randi frowned at Baz. "If I want something, I could go down to the kitchen."

"But since you have not had a tour of the house yet, it would be a chore to find it."

"I'd probably end up falling in the indoor pool," Randi joked.

"Oh, that's unlikely. The pool has a very wide apron," Emilio offered. "But if you would like to go swimming this afternoon, it is heated and ready for use."

"You have an indoor pool?"

"It is half indoor, half outdoor on the back of the house." Baz's eyes warmed with emotion. "My grandfather installed it for my grandmother. She was a keen swimmer year-round."

"Your grandparents live here?"

"They did until their deaths over a decade ago."

"About the same time you were forced to take over the company."

Baz led her up the wide marble staircase. "Two years before. My grandfather would have been very disappointed I didn't go to university."

"I'm sure he was proud of you, regardless." Randi wasn't going to think about why she felt the need to comfort Baz.

The portraits displayed in gilded frames hanging on the wall of the hall they walked along looked old. "Are those your ancestors?"

"They are. The Perez family has been in Madrid since before the Inquisition."

He pushed open a heavy oak door, leading her into a huge bedroom suite, complete with her own sitting room and balcony off the bedroom. One of the doors led to a spa-like bathroom, naturally, and the other into a walk-in closet that could have been used as another small bedroom. She said as much.

Baz nodded. "What are now the walk-in closets used to be sleeping quarters for maids and valets for my ancestors."

"This is pretty impressive for guest accommodations."

"While the guest rooms are perfectly elegant, only two have their own sitting rooms."

"And I got one? I'm honored." She ran her hand over the carving on the canopied four-poster bed. "I can see where Casa Clavel has been updated, but you retained the historic tone to the place. It's wonderful."

"I am glad you like it, but this is the family hall."

"What?" she asked, spinning around to face him. "I'm not family."

"I wanted you close. There was no reason to put you in the guest hall as we are the only people in the hacienda at present."

"But..." There went her plan to keep her distance from him.

"If you do not like this room, we can move you."

"You know it's not the room."

"I am glad to hear that."

"You're really used to getting your own way, aren't you?"

"Is that a bad thing?"

"For me, maybe it is."

"Because I want something you do not?" He removed his suit coat and laid it over a chair that looked like it was original to the house. "You must know I would never push you into anything you found objectionable."

"Like you didn't push me into coming to Spain?" Trick, more like.

Only, if she was honest with herself, she'd admit she wanted a way across the chasm separating them, too. She just didn't know if that desire was going to cause her more pleasure or pain.

CHAPTER ELEVEN

BAZ TUGGED ON his tie, loosening it and then pulling it off. It landed in a neat line over his jacket. "I would not have forced you. You have to know that."

Did she? Honesty compelled her to admit, "I do." She sighed. "I did. As contrary as it may sound, if I'd thought you really were forcing me, I would have refused to come and let the chips fall where they may."

More important, why was he taking off his clothes?

"So you, too, are used to doing as you like." He toed off his shoes, pushing them under the chair with his foot.

"Maybe, but with a lot more limits than you." Should she say something about the slow, casual striptease?

His socks were next, but so far he was keeping the important garments on. "Trust me. A man in my position has many constraints on his life and actions."

She scoffed, "You live like a king." Literally.

"And like any royalty, I have responsibilities to the people who rely on me, to my company, to my family. I am not responsible for the well-being of a nation, but nothing I choose for my life is without consequences for others, sometimes many others. I always remember that."

"You're saying you're not a despot."

"I am a man with a great many responsibilities." He unbuckled his belt and dropped it with the jacket and tie.

"Why are you undressing?" she asked, her voice a little high-pitched.

He shrugged. "I am merely getting comfortable. That is one of the benefits of being home, is it not?"

"Sure, but it wasn't just the desire to be back in your own home that prompted your return to Spain, right? Those responsibilities you were talking about are calling to you, aren't they?"

Her hint seemed to fall on deaf ears as he unbuttoned the top two buttons on his shirt. *"Sí."*

"Do you need to get to work, then?" she asked hopefully.

"Are you trying to get rid of me?" He smiled at her and then took her hand before she had a chance to answer, pulling her toward the French doors leading to the balcony. "I worked on the plane while you napped. I can enjoy some uninterrupted time with you now."

She'd closed her eyes to avoid more deep discussions and had ended up falling asleep, not waking until a few minutes before they landed.

"I haven't been sleeping well," she excused herself.

He nodded like he understood. Maybe he did.

She stepped toward the rail, turning her face up to the sun. "I love fall in a warm climate."

"Oregon's more definitive seasons are not to your liking?"

"The rain is okay, but I don't like being cold. It doesn't get extreme in Portland, like the Midwest. Or so Kayla tells me, but we've had some pretty chilly days already this fall and I know last winter they got snow several days in Portland."

"And there are places covered in snow for six months out of the year."

"I know, but I wouldn't want to live there. I'm a warm baby."

"You were raised in Southern California. That

is understandable. I have never wanted to move to a colder climate, either. A vacation to the snowy mountains is sufficient exposure for me."

"I was starting to miss the sunshine," she admitted. "It was worth it to be close to Kayla, though. It's been great getting to know my sister."

"Why were you raised apart?"

"My mom abandoned her at a truck stop when she was three, before I was born. We didn't even know the other existed until Andreas hired an investigator to find Kayla's family."

Baz's mouth twisted with distaste. "Your mother is a piece of work."

"She is that. I'm nothing like her."

"No, of course not."

"But I could pass her genes on if I have children. Most days I don't think it's worth the risk." Just sometimes, Randi wondered what it would be like to carry a baby inside her.

He brushed the hair away the gentle wind had blown into her face. "You could also pass along your kindness, compassion, intelligence, beauty and strength of character."

"Don't say stuff like that."

"I will not refrain from the truth."

"You're so certain of yourself."

"I know what I want."

"What is that?" she asked, needing him to spell out just what he expected here.

"I want another chance with you."

He'd gone to a lot of trouble for more uncommitted sex from the same partner and she told him so.

"Maybe I desire more than uncommitted sex."

"No. Don't. Don't imply you want something more than that. We both know it would never work."

"You are so certain?"

"Your life is here in Spain. I just started working for my sister's charity. I'm still getting to know her."

"Then let us start with the sex."

"Wha—?"

His lips cut off her words, his hands warm on her hips. And just that fast, Randi's worries and decision to stay away from him physically melted into nothingness.

She'd never responded to another man the way she did him and probably never would again. No matter what he felt for her, she was pretty sure she'd fallen in love with Basilio Perez.

It was too fast. It was unreasonable. It made no kind of sense. Emotions didn't just sprout up and take over a person's heart, but hers was locked down with an emotional craving no one else was ever going to quench.

It didn't have to be logical. She'd fallen. Her feelings were real. So real she knew she was in for a world of pain when she went back to the States and left him to his glittery world of billionaires and beauties.

But right now she could have this. Sex. A connection. And she was going to take it.

Randi was going to wring every ounce of pleasure out of the next two weeks that she could get. The one thing she wasn't going to do, though, was ever admit her feelings to a man who had declared with conviction that he didn't buy into the romantic love concept.

Besides, you had to trust someone to admit your love for them, to let it spill over and infect every area of your life. And Randi still didn't trust Baz.

Baz's kiss turned heated, the exploratory nature disappearing almost immediately when she responded with unfettered passion.

He lifted her up, helping her to wrap her legs around him, and carried her, still kissing back, into the bedroom.

Randi laughed, reveling in the pleasure of his

touch as he dropped her onto the bed. "You've got a real caveman streak."

"I have been called primitive more than once."

"By other lovers?" she wondered, not really wanting an answer.

"No. I have never had trouble with control with another woman. Not like I do with you. My past liaisons have always been very civilized."

"I wouldn't call you civilized in bed." Far from it. Her voice caught as he began stripping the smart suit she'd worn for travel off her body.

It was not her usual look, not nearly casual enough, but she'd wanted armor when she saw him early this morning, and the suit had been necessary. Now she just wanted the tailored jacket and pencil skirt off. Her fingers fumbled with the tiny buttons on the blouse until Baz took hold of both sides and jerked it open, buttons popping, fabric tearing.

His urgency turned her on even more, making her ache for his touch in her most intimate places. He stopped and just stared down at her lingerie. "Did you wear this for me?"

"You know I like to wear pretty underwear."

His espresso gaze heated, singeing her with its

intensity. "*Sí*, but you had to know I would get you out of that prim and proper suit."

"No, that wasn't the plan." At least in her conscious mind.

She was honest enough to admit, to herself at least, that her subconscious may well have had different ideas.

"Oh, it was always the plan. I would have had you on the plane if you hadn't looked so peaceful sleeping."

"You're arrogant."

"And?"

"On the verge of losing out on a good thing if you get too cocky." So, that? Was a total lie.

She wasn't stopping what they were doing for anything. Her body craved his. Her heart craved whatever connection she could have before walking away.

If there was emotional pain mixed with her incandescent pleasure, Randi was a big girl. She could handle it.

She had plenty experience in that regard.

"We would not want that."

"No…" She gasped as his hot mouth landed on her curve above the line of her aqua satin demi bra.

His tongue ran along the edge of her bra, branding her with the oral caress.

Oh, man. She had no resistance to his touch. Even the slightest connection between their bodies had her ready for the deepest of intimacy. Had he pressed, they would have joined the Mile-High Club on the way over from Portland.

His short breaths, the way his hands were so urgent on her body, said he was just as susceptible to her.

Baz pushed the demi bra down and suddenly hot, wet suction engulfed her nipple, sending pleasure down her body, right into the core of her.

"Yes, Baz, please…"

His hands worked at getting rid of the rest of their clothes while he continued to pleasure her with his mouth. Her body bowed upward, electric impulses making her muscles contract with the overwhelming bliss.

When they were both completely naked, her last bits of clothing peeled away with passion-imbued reverence, he stopped and just stared at her, the waning fall sun casting his olive skin in a golden glow. "You are so perfect."

She shook her head. "Hardly."

"Sí. Perfección."

"Saying it in Spanish doesn't make it any more true."

"I want you, *cariña*. I have never been in bed with a woman I found so enthralling. No other woman has ever drawn me like you do."

"How can that be true?"

"I don't know." His tone and expression said he really didn't. "But it is."

"What we have in bed is special."

"So I've been telling you."

"Show me."

"It will be my pleasure."

Only the minute he started kissing her body again, his hands busy caressing spots he'd taught her were unexpected erogenous zones, she realized she didn't want to just lie there and accept the delight he brought to her body. She wanted to do some touching of her own.

Lots and lots of touching.

Randi pushed against Baz's shoulder until he lifted his head and torso so she could press him onto his back. Then it was her turn to taste his body, to map his rock-hard muscles with her fingertips.

"What are you doing to me, *mi hermosa*?"

"Whatever I want." It was nothing less than the truth.

Regardless of what had happened between them, she felt more freedom to explore with this man than she ever had with her two previous lovers.

Baz didn't try to give directions. He didn't subtly encourage her to move one way or another with his own body. No, he let her kiss him, first on the lips then on every sexy hollow and dip on his gorgeous, masculine body.

When she wrapped her fingers around his hot and oh, so hard erection, his groan was all the encouragement she needed to keep doing what she wanted. She caressed him with inexpert but enthusiastic movements before sliding down his body so she could take him into her mouth.

The sound he made then was primitive and full of male need.

She would have smiled in triumph, but her mouth was full. She did her best to take as much as she could between her lips, breathing through her nose when he bumped the back of her throat. She kept an up and down motion with her hand on his rigid column of flesh.

Suddenly, he was pulling her head away from

his sex, his breathing harsh. "I don't want to come in your mouth."

She didn't ask why not because she wanted the same thing he did. Him inside her.

He pulled her up until she straddled him. "Are you ready for me?"

"Yes."

"Put this on me." He handed her a condom.

She didn't ask where it came from. Right then, Randi didn't care.

She tore open the packet with her teeth and then pulled out the thin latex circle. Concentrating so her hands did not shake too badly, passion riding her hard, she rolled the protection down over his straining erection.

He moaned as her hand slid down with the latex. "Yes, Miranda, *cariña*, that is so good."

She loved the way even this act was part of the pleasure.

Baz grabbed her hips, and in an arousing feat of strength, he lifted her up until her labia kissed the head of his latex-covered erection. Then he guided her down, centimeter by slow centimeter as he rocked upward with slow, steady movements, until he was seated completely inside her.

They both froze for several seconds. For her

part, Randi was simply overwhelmed by sensation. Baz had an expression on his handsome features she was afraid to trust, but his dark gaze bored into hers with profound emotion.

"This between us, this is too good, too special, too important, to simply dismiss."

She nodded, unable to deny the truth of his words.

His hips canted once, then twice, both of them gasping at the increased sensation until desire for him took over even the soul-deep emotion and she had to move.

Baz's eyes closed for a second, the rictus of pleasure on his face telling her better than words could how much he was enjoying her riding him.

Then his eyelids opened, revealing a gaze almost black with pleasure, and his hands came up her body to cup her breasts. He kneaded the modest curves, expertly playing with nipples already engorged with blood and sensitized by his earlier touch.

Randi shifted her angle and suddenly his big sex was caressing that spot inside her that sent jolts of ecstasy throughout her body. Bliss coiled tight inside her, waves of pleasure emanating from her womb until she knew her climax was imminent.

"That's right, *mi amor*." He thrust up against her, increasing Randi's pleasure. "Move just like that."

She wasn't about to stop but didn't have the breath to tell him so. She found her breath a moment later, though, in order to let loose a scream of ecstasy when one of his hands slid down her body until his thumb could brush against her swollen clitoris. Just like that, the pleasure inside her detonated, explosions of bliss making her muscles contract. Her heart beat so fast she could barely breathe, and her cry of completion choked off by more of the same.

He kept moving under her, even as she fell forward against him, his thumb prolonging her moment of annihilating pleasure.

Still hard inside her, Baz stilled, his hands locked onto her thighs so she couldn't move, either. "So good, *mi cariña*."

"You didn't come."

His smile was all sexy, confident male. "I am not finished with you yet."

"What?" She felt finished.

But then he moved under her, sending jolts of electric bliss sparking along her nerve endings, and she thought, maybe not.

The expression on his handsome Spanish features was nothing short of devilish as he rolled them, his shifting body inside her sending more aftershocks through Randi.

He kissed her for long minutes, but then he withdrew from her body completely.

She protested until he moved down her body to bury his mouth between her legs. As his tongue flicked out to barely touch her clitoris, she found herself panting with renewed pleasure. He kept the touches featherlight for several minutes until she found her body moving to meet the tantalizing caresses. Then he increased the pressure, his finger pressing up inside her even as he nibbled against her swollen bundle of nerves.

Baz showed her that when it came to giving pleasure with his mouth he was a master, drawing forth a second, even stronger, climax from her before he surged up her body to push inside her again.

Tears ran hotly down her temples as the pleasure and the emotional intensity of their physical connection overwhelmed Randi.

He brushed at the wetness with his fingertips. "You are mine, *hermosa*. Made especially for my body to connect to yours."

She couldn't think of anything to say; she was

too raw from what was happening between them, but she wouldn't have denied his claim if she *could* make her brain-to-mouth function work.

He plunged in and out of her, finally losing his vaunted control, driving them both higher and higher, words of praise in his native tongue dripping from his lips.

Her throat raw from screaming, Randi climaxed for a third time, this time taking him over the precipice of pleasure with her, his hoarse shout triumphant.

He kissed her possessively, intense passion coming through the way his lips moved so adamantly over hers. After long moments of him telling her a story with his lips against hers, the kiss gentled until finally, he broke the connection, pulling carefully from her body.

"I must take care of this." He waved his hand toward the condom now covering his semierect sex.

She couldn't even work up the energy to move a single finger, much less shift her body. "Okay."

He came back to the bed and lifted her into his arms.

"Where are we going?" she asked, her postcoital lethargy making her not really care what his answer was. She found a secret part of herself that thoroughly enjoyed his caveman tendencies and not a single bit of energy to protest it.

"My bed, where you belong, *mi amor.*"

That was the second time he'd called her that. His love. She knew he didn't mean it the way she wanted him to, but his use of it now… It meant something. Didn't it?

True to his word, he carried her naked body out of the room and down the hall to the room next door. She should have guessed he would be so close by. If anything, his private suite was even more decadent than the one she'd been assigned.

She took in her surroundings with sleepy eyes as he carried her through to the bedroom and then maneuvered into his bed, climbing in with her and wrapping her in his arms.

"I shouldn't be tired," she slurred. "Slept on the plane."

"I've worn you out." Pride infused his voice.

She couldn't take him to task for it. He was right. Randi let her eyes slide shut and snuggled into Baz's body. She would work on shoring her defenses against him later.

CHAPTER TWELVE

THE FOLLOWING DAYS settled into a pattern.

Randi and Baz shared breakfast each morning before he left for his office. Then she spent a few hours answering emails and going over things for Kayla's for Kids that weren't impacted by the time difference.

Somehow Mr. Billionaire Business Mogul had managed to work short days for the entire two weeks Randi had been there. He came back to the hacienda for a late lunch, which Randi waited to eat with him. Afterward, he took her sightseeing, introducing her to his favorite places in and around Madrid as well as full-on tourist traps.

She was totally entranced by the Royal Palace. No wonder he considered his hacienda just a home. Spain's palace in Madrid was the biggest royal palace in Europe, its Sabatini and Campo del Moro Gardens beyond beautiful. She wanted to go back before she left Madrid, but then she would really enjoy revisiting Almudena Cathedral, the Prado Museum and the Alcalá Gate again, too.

In the evenings they each spent another couple of hours working, when their contacts in North America would be awake and at their own desks. Afterward, they had a late dinner, sometimes in the glamorous hacienda dining room, sometimes at Michelin Star restaurants, and a couple of times they had amazing food at hole-in-the-wall eateries she would never expect Baz to frequent. But always, always, they ended up back in Baz's bed, making love into the wee hours of the morning, their passion never waning.

Every day the life she was living in Spain became more and more the life she *wanted* to live. And that was a very dangerous mind-set.

Two days before she was supposed to fly home, Randi went looking for Baz in his office. He'd set her up at a beautiful desk in the Casa Clavel library. Filled with books and populated with furniture his family had collected over the centuries, the room was rich with history. And she loved it. Baz's study was through a connecting door, and Randi liked how close he was while they worked together in the evenings, too.

He was on the phone, so she sat down to wait

until he was done, more than a little confused by the two phone calls she'd just had.

Baz's dark gaze flared with pleasure at the sight of her and he smiled when she sat down, putting a finger up to tell her he would only be a minute.

She nodded, smiling back, for once doing nothing to hide or suppress how pleased she was to be near him.

His eyes widened in surprise, his mouth dropping open in shock. He had to visibly collect himself before he ended his call with an abruptness that surprised *her*.

"To what do I owe this pleasure?" He stood up and came around the big, ornate desk that he'd told her had been a gift to one of his ancestors from King Carlos III.

Baz moved close to Randi like he was irresistibly drawn to her.

She knew the feeling. It was all Randi could do to stay in her chair. "I've just had a couple of very interesting calls."

He cocked his head to the side like he had no idea what she was talking about.

"I was going over the final purchase details for the new facility with the broker."

"Si?" Still, Baz looked like he had no idea where this was going.

"He was confused about the *gift* of the furnishings to the shelter. In fact, he said *we* were paying for them, which I knew we weren't doing. Or at least I thought I did."

"Oh."

"Yes, oh. Apparently, there is a special account that has been set aside to pay for the furnishings as well as any renovations that need to be made on the facility."

Baz shrugged. "Kayla's for Kids is a more than worthy endeavor."

"So, you did donate the two million dollars sitting in that account?"

"I did."

"Why didn't you tell me?"

"I didn't want you to refuse the gift because you were angry with me."

"It was for the shelter, not for me. You must have realized I would appreciate your generosity."

"I didn't want you to appreciate my money."

No. Baz wanted Randi to appreciate *him*. And the way she'd smiled at him when she came into the study had so shocked him, he'd cut off a business call to find out why she'd done it.

She gave in to the need to stand up and walked over to him, initiating contact like she never did, stepping into his personal space, placing her hands on his chest. "You're a really amazing guy, Basilio Perez."

"Because I gave the shelter some money?" he asked, not sounding particularly happy by that thought.

She leaned up and kissed the underside of his chiseled jaw. "Because you kept it a secret, because you didn't use it to try to get on my good side."

His arms came around her and he dipped his head and kissed her full on the mouth, his tongue playing with the seam of her lips before he lifted his head to say, "I'm very glad I finally did something right."

"You did more than one thing. You're paying for the new shelter liaison. Kayla said she's not coming out of the shelter's budget, but that she has a two-year contract."

"I would like to accept your appreciation, but hiring Mrs. Patel was purely selfish on my part. I wanted you to be free to travel with me when necessary. To perhaps even relocate here."

Her heart nearly exploded in her chest. "You want me to move to Spain?"

"*Sí.*"

"But why?"

"Because I cannot make Portland my permanent place of residence. While Perez Holdings is an international company, my support staff, my best acquisition groups, they are all here in Spain."

"You want something long-term with me," she realized, bemused.

He stared at her like she'd lost her mind. "Do you think I went to such efforts for a few more nights of sex, even incredible sex?"

"But…you said…no commitment." Her thoughts came out in disjointed little bursts.

"No, *mi amor. You* said no commitment and refused to believe anything else. Has this past week felt like no commitment?" His hands pressed into her lower back, bringing their bodies together.

"I…" How could she answer that? It *had* felt casual, but she was beginning to realize that was because she hadn't allowed herself to consider anything else. Because it had also felt like the beginning of a life together. "So to be clear, you're saying you want a relationship with me?"

"With a view to marriage, *sí.*"

"Marriage?" she squeaked.

"What else? I will never be content to see you with another man. I hope you would be bothered by the idea of me being with another woman."

"Um…yes." It would gut her. Which was one of the reasons she was glad he lived in Spain.

"But what about my sister? The shelter."

"I currently travel to the States every couple of months. I could up that schedule to once a month, or at least every six weeks."

"You would do that?"

"I'm already looking at properties to open a Loving Sisters Shelter here in Madrid."

"I've never heard of that organization."

"That's because it is a new name for a multinational nonprofit run by you and your sister, focused on the welfare of children and youth."

"What? No…we didn't… You're looking at facilities?"

"I have found three prospects, two in the city center, and one on the outskirts of Madrid I was hoping you'd look at next week."

"Next week? But I was supposed to fly home the day after tomorrow."

"I was hoping to convince you to stay longer.

Things have been working out, haven't they? You like living here."

"You're serious about this, aren't you?"

"I am serious about you."

"Baz, I think you might love me." She couldn't believe she'd blurted it out like that.

His face closed up, pain flaring briefly in his eyes. "If I don't?"

"Whatever you feel for me is enough." She didn't need perfection. She didn't need him to give voice to feelings that he was clearly not ready to deal with yet.

And might never be.

The *perfect* relationship was a fantasy anyway. She knew that. Even Andreas and Kayla had their issues. All couples did. But they fit. They loved each other and that wouldn't be any less valid without the words.

"You are sure? You'll stay?" His smile was incandescent. "You have forgiven me for deceiving you in the beginning?"

"Yes." To all of it.

He began moving toward the settee against the wall. "I believe we need to celebrate."

"Champagne?"

"How about champagne sex, fizzy and delicious?"

"You're quite the romantic."

"If you say so."

"I do."

The kissing and touching that followed had a vulnerable quality to it that neither had shown the other to this point. She straddled his thighs as he sat naked on the brocade-covered sofa. "Do you have a condom?"

"In my desk drawer."

She gave him a look.

"I put them there the day after I brought you here."

"So you don't have sex with women in your office."

"I have never had sex with any other women anywhere in my home. This hacienda is my refuge."

She kissed him for such a good answer and then climbed off him to retrieve the condom. He groaned and tried to hold on to her, making them both laugh.

They made love, her body encasing his, her hips moving in a rhythm that maximized both their pleasure. He kissed her, over and over again, his hands kneading her backside, his hips thrusting up to meet hers. They came together, her cry and his groan muffled by their kiss.

Armand Perez returned to Casa Clavel the following week, exhibiting nothing but delight at the news that his son and Randi were now an official couple.

"Will you be moving to Spain permanently, or will you try to make this work long distance?" Armand asked over dinner the first night of his return.

Randi swallowed, not sure how she wanted to answer that. She'd told Baz she would stay with her *yes*, but knew he hadn't been clear she was answering all his questions with the single word. She'd realized that later by something he said.

Now Baz looked at her, waiting for her answer to his father's question, as interested as Armand. Only Baz's gaze held vulnerability as well as cautious expectation. It was the vulnerability and caution that helped her give her answer, to make it official.

She smiled at Armand. "We are going to look at spots for a possible shelter tomorrow."

"That is good. Our Madrid children can always use another advocate."

"You *are* moving here?" Baz asked, looking for confirmation she was happy to give him.

"I'll call Kayla after dinner and let her know. Last week I just told her I was staying longer." Maybe Randi hadn't been all that sure of her decision, but she was now. "I think she'll like the idea of expanding Kayla's for Kids to Loving Sisters Shelter."

Randi was right. Her sister loved the idea of going international with the services for displaced and at-risk children. She wasn't as keen on Randi living in Spain.

"I'm going to miss you."

"Baz said we'll come to America once a month, at least every six weeks. You and Andreas can visit us in Spain, as well."

"Once a month? You promise?"

"Some visits you'll have to meet me in California, so I can see Dad and the grandparents."

"Of course I will. Oh, Randi. I'm so happy it's working out between you, but don't you think maybe you're moving fast?"

"Yes. It is fast. Yes, it is scary, but it feels right. More than right, it feels necessary. I trust him."

"Really? Even after?"

"Partly because of what he did. Baz is the kind of guy who will do whatever it takes to keep his family safe. That will include me."

"You're already talking marriage?" Kayla shrieked.

"Not every corporate shark takes six years to figure out that the best woman in the world for him is already taking up space in his life."

Kayla laughed. "Yeah, Andreas was pretty blind. He's not anymore, though."

"Yeah, I've noticed."

When the phone rang an hour later, as Randi and Baz were preparing for bed, Kayla's name flashed on the screen along with the picture of her gorgeous smile. Randi grabbed the phone. "Hey, sis, what's up?"

"Have you been keeping up on the Google alert for your name?"

"What? No, actually. Baz took care of stuff before I left. I've enjoyed not having to track my name and wonder if today would be the day I'd get vilified in the press again." Her heart tightened, her stomach cramping. "Are you saying Carl Madison went back on the agreement?"

That fast Baz was there, putting his hand out for the phone. She gave it to him without a second thought.

"Kayla, it is Basilio. What is going on?"

He grimaced, listening to whatever Kayla was saying, his expression turning more and more grim as her sister's agitated tones came through the phone.

Finally, he said, "Do not worry about it, Kayla. I will take care of it."

Kayla said something.

"No, of course not."

She said something else.

His lips tilted in a partial smile. "Thank you. We will see you soon."

They ended the call.

"Didn't she want to talk to me again?" Randi asked.

"She understood I needed to tell you the latest development."

"What latest development?"

Baz pulled her over to their bed and helped her climb inside before joining her, his arm a solid presence around her waist as they faced each other.

He traced her jawbone and then tucked her hair behind Randi's ear. "I do not want you to worry."

"Just tell me."

"The researchers at the television station you were going to do the interview on are much better at their job than any media outlet so far. They got ahold of the police reports, both from five years ago and recently when Carlos assaulted you."

"What? How?" Agitated and worried, she plucked at the bedding. "I didn't say anything. I didn't even hint. I promise, Baz. Andreas's contact set up the interview and no one knew exactly what I planned to say, just that I was going to give my side of the story."

"Of course you didn't. You have too much integrity to go back on your word."

"That's what you told Kayla. That of course I hadn't done it," Randi said wonderingly.

"Naturally."

She threw herself at Baz. "I love you so much. I know you don't believe in it, but I'm not keeping the words inside."

His arms automatically wrapped around her, pulling her tight against his near-naked body. "Because I believe in your integrity?"

"Because everything. You're ruthless, but you

weren't lying when you said it was both with and on behalf of your family. You're kind. You're generous even if you'd like to hide that fact. You're incredibly loyal. And, well, you're sexier than any other man alive."

"I believe you are profoundly biased."

"That's the way it's supposed to be. In love."

He got a strange look on his face. "Love. I promised myself that I would never fall for that construct."

"I'm allowed to love you, whatever promises you've made to yourself. You'd better accept that now. We won't be talking marriage if you don't." That was a deal-breaker for her. It was one thing to accept a man who never said the words, but exhibited the emotion; another thing entirely to expect her never to speak of her love for him.

He smiled wryly. "I broke the promise."

"What? What are you saying?" She cuddled closer to him, looking up into his espresso gaze, tendrils of hope curling around her heart and seeping into her soul.

"I'm saying that the only thing that explains what we have between us, my need not only to have you in my bed, but also in my life, and not just for now, but for the rest of that life..." He stopped speaking, just looking down at her, his dark eyes filled with wonder, warmth and a lot of heat. "I love you, Miranda. You have broken through every chain locking my heart tight."

Tears filled her eyes. "I didn't think you'd ever admit it to yourself, much less me."

"How can I show less courage than you?"

"I'm not brave."

"Despite all you have experienced, you believe in the goodness in people. You believe you can make a difference in the lives of children. You trust me. That is a gift of the highest magnitude."

"I love when you start talking all formal."

"It is easier when my emotions are trying to take over my brain, especially when I'm not communicating in the language of my birth."

"I thought you didn't do powerful emotion."

"I find that I do."

The tears spilled over. "Oh, Baz."

"I love you, now and forever." He rolled her under him.

She smiled up into his handsome face. "Into eternity."

EPILOGUE

Carlos threw a fit when Basilio called him about the truth coming out, but ultimately agreed to do what his younger brother instructed.

He didn't want to lose the support of Perez Holdings. Between his PR team and the one dedicated to Perez Holdings, they mitigated as much damage as possible. But this time around the truth was out there for everyone to judge.

Tiffany ended up taking an extended holiday in Australia; the children came to Spain to stay with Basilio, Miranda and Armand. Miranda was glad to be out of the US while the story got a chance to blow over. She refused all requests for interviews, photo ops or anything else that might put her into the public eye.

She was ridiculously content in Basilio's home and his life, her days busy with the children, her duties with Kayla's for Kids and the new Loving Sisters Shelter. Miranda found peace unlike she'd known in five years as she grew closer to Grace and Jamie, the little boy who had not only survived the accident, but now flourished with keen intelligence and typical little-boy enthusiasm for life.

When they returned the children to the States two weeks later, it was to learn that Kayla was pregnant.

She and her beautiful son attended Miranda and Baz's wedding the following year. The infant, too small to take part in the ceremony, sat on his proud *papá*'s lap. The little girl they had adopted out of foster care, however, was just the right age to act as a flower girl. She stood beside her mother and Miranda as she and Baz spoke vows of love and lifelong commitment. It was only afterward she learned that Baz had hired security to keep her mother away from her special day.

He took protecting Miranda very seriously and spoke of his love for her every day. She was always eager to return the words, truly content, knowing she was genuinely and always safe for the first time in her life.

* * * * *